Insanity Series Book 6

CHECKMATE

by Cameron Jace

Other Books by Cameron Jace

Checkmate (Book 6)

TABLE OF CONTENTS

Prologue Part One

World Chess Championship, Moscow, Russia

The presidents and prime ministers of the world were gathered in the auditorium. They'd come for a global event. They were raising money for citizens who'd recently lost their homes, unable to pay the mortgage and piling bills, and eventually going mad.

The audience clapped with enthusiasm and proudly waved their country's flags in the air, hailing and praising world leaders for caring, then showering them with roses and lilies and praying for them.

The presidents stood proudly and blew kisses in the air, pretending to be modest and humble, while they secretly laughed at their citizens. Because, in reality, it was the presidents and prime ministers themselves who'd caused those bills and pushed citizens to the verge of insanity. They were both the killer and judge, which was madly beautiful.

And what better way to raise money but a chess event, where they played games on TV, the same way they played with their own people in real life?

The world leaders sat, each at their own small table with a single chessboard upon it. Silence swooped over the auditorium as they began to organize their chess pieces. Of course, all the leaders chose the color white for the game.

Over one hundred and thirty presidents and prime ministers were ready to play. The idea was to accept donations with every move they made in the game. But the trickiest part was that they weren't going to play against each other. They were going to play against one man.

Yes, you read that right. All the world leaders were playing against one man. They called him the Chessmaster, a genius Russian player who'd never lost a game.

"Did he really never lose a game?" the American president hissed at the British prime minister next to him.

"Shhh," the British prime minister said. They called him Mr. Paperwhite because he only dressed in white paper instead of clothes. "Be silent. This isn't an American football game."

The American president rolled his eyes. The British were a bit too conservative at times. He turned to his left, facing another world leader by the name of King Dick, a flamboyant dictator who ruled a poor third world country with wealthy leaders, each of them richer than Bill Gates and Ali Baba combined.

"Hey," the American president said. "Is it true the Chessmaster never lost a game?"

"What do you care?" King Dick breathed onto his recently manicured fingernails. "Americans can't play chess anyways. You'll lose no matter what."

Mr. Paperwhite snickered at that comment.

"Neither can the Brits," King Dick mocked him, and the British prime minister's face flushed red. "Only the Russians are good at chess. And the best of the Russians is the Chessmaster."

"But how can he never lose a game?" The American president gritted his teeth. "We Americans are big on winning. We're always number one. But even so, we have to lose a game once in a while."

"That's because you're not as good as the Chessmaster," King Dick said. "Didn't you ever hear about him winning the maddest game in the world?"

"Maddest game?" The American president leaned forward. "With whom?"

King Dick looked sideways then also leaned closer, his eyes bulging. "The Chessmaster is so good that it's said that he won a game he played with..." He shrugged.

"With whom?" The American president's eyes widened.

King Dick pointed upward. "With God himself."

"God plays chess?" Mr. Paperwhite questioned from behind.

"Of course he plays chess. He is God. He can play everything." The American president elbowed the prime minister back and said to King Dick, "Did God really lose a game to the Russian Chessmaster? How?"

"He cheated," King Dick said, cupping his mouth with a hand.

"Of course. That's it," Mr. Paperwhite said. "You only beat God if you cheat."

"You don't get it," King Dick said. "It was God who cheated first."

"Get outta here!" The American president almost gasped.

"It's what the myth says." King Dick nodded. "The Chessmaster is too good. God had to cheat."

"But how did the Chessmaster win that game?" Mr. Paperwhite asked.

"The Chessmaster cheated back, of course," the American president said, gritting his teeth again. "Tell me, King Dick, does this mean that the Chessmaster knows God personally?"

"They don't play golf together on Sundays, but of course he does," King Dick said. "Why are you asking?"

"I am wondering if the Chessmaster could introduce me to him. We could have brunch in the White House. God and I."

"Why would the American president want to meet with God?" Mr. Paperwhite mocked him. "He will send you straight to hell."

"Hell is negotiable," the American president said. "We could always fix a deal."

"Then why do you want to meet God?" King Dick asked. "You're not even good at chess."

"You want to know why?" the American president said, smirking. "Imagine I knew God personally. Oh boy, we could do some business."

Suddenly the host of the event interrupted the conversation, tapping his microphone, and the three world leaders straightened in their chairs.

"Ladies and gentlemen," the host announced. "I'm proud to present the man who never lost a chess game!" He waved his hands in the air and the crowd hailed. "The man who is about to play against one hundred and thirty world leaders at the same time—and promises he will win."

The crowd was going crazy.

"The man who played with God himself and won," the host continued. "Russia's proudest son, the Chessmaster himself."

And there, the Chessmaster appeared from behind the red curtains. To the three leaders' surprise, the Chessmaster looked like nothing they had expected.

Prologue Part Two

World Chess Championship, Moscow, Russia

The Chessmaster was an old man. Partially bald, with flapping, uncombed, and stiff white hair sticking to the side of his head, even worse than Einstein's. He had a small forehead, small eyes, but a long bridge of a nose. He was beardless, but had an unusual mustache. A handlebar mustache that stretched sideways and curved upward like an eagle ready to take off.

He didn't laugh, but he looked funny somehow. He looked childish, and as if he had a short attention span. In fact, he didn't pay any attention to the audience. His eyes were focused on the chessboards he was about to raid with his unmatchable talents.

But one thing really stood out. The Chessmaster didn't wear normal clothes. Not even weird ones. He wore the silver armor of a knight, just like his favorite chess piece.

Chin up, he strode toward his first opponent, the American president, and nodded, implying he wanted the president to make the first move.

The president was infatuated with the Chessmaster, though he never expected him to look the way he did, and moved a pawn two blocks ahead.

The Chessmaster stared at the pawn with an expressionless face, then slightly raised his head to meet the president's eyes.

"In how many moves do you want to lose?" the Chessmaster said in a cold voice that was as grey as cold souls. Appearances aside, this wasn't a man to make fun of.

"I don't want to lose," the president said. "I want to win."

"Who do you think you are?" The Chessmaster leaned over, hands behind his back. "Rocky Balboa in a Hollywood movie where you beat the Russian champion in the end?"

The crowd, mostly Europeans and Russians, laughed.

"I didn't mean to insult you," the president said, "but I want to win."

"Fine with me." The Chessmaster said. "If you want to win, drink one of the vodka shots next to the chessboard."

The president hadn't noticed the tiny vodka glasses lined up next to the chessboard. Seven glasses on each side. Seven for him. Seven for his opponent.

"It's a Russian custom," the Chessmaster said. "Make a chess move and take a vodka drink."

"What's the point?" the president asked.

"Each vodka shot will make you dizzier and compromise your judgment, so it gets harder to play along."

"I see," the president said. "If I do it, then I will have a chance to win?"

"A chance, yes," the Chessmaster said, "but I never lose."

The American president gulped the vodka. It was bitter, and it hammered his head so hard his cheeks reddened and his spine tingled.

The Chessmaster laughed at him. "This is going to be fun," he said, addressing the hundred and thirty world leaders. "Now each of you has to drink after his chess move. That's the rule. Let's see what happens first. Will you get drunk before you lose the game, or lose the game before you get drunk?"

And so the Chessmaster began to play against each leader, one after the other. It only took him a glance at the chessboard to make his move, while it took each opponent no less than an hour to pick his.

The crowd bit their nails with excitement, though most of the game was in utter silence.

It seemed that the Chessmaster was keen on playing the Pope's representative, an Italian man who represented the Vatican. He'd replaced the Pope because the Pope didn't drink vodka, and none of them previously knew of the drinking rule while playing chess. Though the *New York Times* had claimed the Pope refused to play because God had told him not to, being angry at the Chessmaster beating him earlier.

Who believed newspapers, anyways?

As the games advanced, world leaders began to sweat, taking their time with each move. All but the Pope's representative, who looked in a hurry, picking a move and gulping his shot.

"That's your sixth shot," the Chessmaster told the man. "I'm impressed you've gotten this far without me beating you."

"I win if I drink the seventh shot without you beating me, right?" The religious man smirked like a drunk on the street.

"You win, yes," the Chessmaster said. "But——"

The man eagerly picked a seventh move and gulped his last drink. He let out a strong noise from his throat and stood up, raising his hand with victory. "I beat the Chessmaster!"

"You must be smarter than God." The Chessmaster smiled at the shocked crowd. They couldn't believe the best chess player in the world was losing. Not so easily, or…?

The Pope's representative began to choke and stiffen. The world leaders watched him grow more and more flushed, reddened and unable to breathe.

"Oh," the Chessmaster began, "I forgot to tell you that the vodka is poisoned. It's the kind of poison that kills you once you drink the seventh shot. You could survive drinking six, but you'd be very sick."

"What?" Mr. Paperwhite protested.

"You see, you have to beat me in six moves or you will die," the Chessmaster announced. "And look at you, all the presidents and leaders of the world in one room. I may kill you all tonight. Isn't that frabjous?"

Everyone stared at the madman with horror in their eyes, unable to believe what was happening. Why did the Chessmaster want to kill the leaders of the world? Who was he working for?

The Chessmaster didn't answer any of these questions. He returned to staring at the choking man while pulling at his handlebar mustache. One stroke to the right. One stroke to the left.

Then he made his last move in the game. The move that killed the queen. He nudged the queen piece with the back of his middle finger and watched the Pope's representative drop dead to his knees, and then stroked his mustache, saying, "Checkmate. Who's next?"

Chapter 1

Mr. Jay's limousine, Oxford

I am sitting in the dark of the limousine, not quite sure of what I am doing. It still puzzles me why I agreed to go meet Mr. Jay, whoever he really is. Maybe somewhere inside my mad brain I am still me—a loyal member of Black Chess.

Rocking to the bumps in the road, I don't try to ask questions or make conversation with the unseen passengers inside. I already have so much on my mind. Forget about the choices and decisions for now. I still need to know why I had to kill everyone on the bus in the past. What was the purpose of doing so? Why was it essential to Black Chess that every student on it died?

I take a deep breath, also thinking about what happened to me after the circus. I am sure I saw the gathering of the Inklings in Lewis Carroll's studio when I had my vision in the Garden of Cosmic Speculation. Lewis, the March Hare, Fabiola, Jack, and me. And the little girl; who was she? Most important is: when and how did I change and become the Bad Alice? What happened to me?

"Mr. Jay will be pleased to meet you," the woman in the dark tells me.

I say nothing. What's to say? I don't say I am pleased to meet him too, but I have questions that are eating at me.

"He has always believed in you," she continues. "Never has he doubted that you would embrace the darkness inside you."

"Did he say that? I mean, most people think they are on the good side of the scale, even when they are the most evil."

"Not Mr. Jay. He loves evil, embraces it, and is proud of it. That's why he is the head of Black Chess. But you must know that."

"I haven't remembered everything yet." I play along. "But I am sure it will come to me. Can you remind me what Black Chess really wants?"

"That, you will have to remember for yourself. We never talk about it."

"Ah, we're after the Six Impossible Keys." I am pulling her leg.

"Not exactly. We're after what the Six Keys are for."

"Of course," I say. "Can't wait to remember. How long until we arrive?"

"Not much longer," she says. "We should be there in about—"

Her words are chopped off by a sudden crash against the vehicle. It's a deafening echo of metal scraping against metal.

"What the hell?" she says, panicking.

I try to grip something in the backseat, but there isn't anything, so I rock to the left and smash my head against the window. The blood on my forehead alerts me of the fact that the car is flipping over, and looking outside the limo's window, I realize we're on the edge of a cliff.

Chapter 2

Darkness and panic aren't good friends at all. The unseen men and women inside the limousine are screaming and the smell of blood is making me nauseated. I have no idea what's happening. I can only see outside the limo, but not inside. I'm not really sure how this is possible, but I am not going to argue with death knocking at the door right now.

"We're about to fall off the cliff," the woman screams in the dark.

"No shit," I mumble, surprised with her lack of grit when she is working for the darkest organization on earth. "Hey, driver! Unlock the doors."

"I think he is dead, and the car has security locks to keep you inside," the woman says. "Those were Mr. Jay's orders, since he suspected this would happen."

"You think I did this?" I snap, but try not to move as the car begins to ease over the gravel underneath, skewing toward the cliff. "I just met you on the street. No one knows I am meeting Mr. Jay."

"How about the Pillar?" The woman grunts.

The suggestion makes me feel better. Who knew? Now that she mentioned the Pillar may have caused the accident, I find myself feeling better.

"But don't think we'll let him save you," she says. "The limo has an emergency system. Reds are on their way. They should be here before your stupid caterpillar comes."

The car takes another heavy jolt and the others in the limo panic again. I don't. I try to see if I can kick the glass open without affecting the car's balance. I am not going to die in Black Chess's limo.

And even if it's the Pillar who planned the accident, I am not going to wait for him to save me.

"Shut up!" I tell the others, carefully crawling toward the window.

The car seems stable, so I get closer, now thinking of what to break the window with.

Peeking outside, I can't locate where we are. There is a river below the cliff, but it's unrecognizable to me.

A sudden bang freezes me in place. However, the car isn't moving. Then I hear a couple of footsteps on the roof.

"It's him," the woman says. "The Pillar!" She grabs me by the neck, trying to choke me. "I won't let him have you."

I struggle, fighting her while the car bounces in every direction. "Stop it or we'll die." I elbow her in the face and hear her scream.

The car's window suddenly breaks, its shattered glass splinters inward, and I have to shield my face with my hands.

"Damn you, Pillar!" the woman shouts.

A smile forms on my face when I glimpse the Pillar's shadowy hand stretching toward me.

I stretch mine back, but when I do, I am shocked to find it's not the Pillar. In fact, it's a Red.

The woman laughs behind me. "Told you my men will get you first."

Chapter 3

Margaret Kent's private mansion,
Kensington, London

Margaret Kent was staring at her son's picture, counting the days until she'd have him back from the Queen of Hearts. The vicious Queen who stopped at nothing to get her hands on the Six Impossible Keys.

Margaret gasped. It had been a long and painful road to find her son. And it seemed like it was only getting longer. She prayed that her plan would work out in the end, and she decided to start by answering her private phone that had been ringing all morning.

"Yes?" She picked up, doing her best to sound collected and as brutal as she'd like everyone to think of her.

"It's me," the voice said. "Carolus."

"What do you want? Didn't I say I'm taking the day off?"

"It's important. I have someone who wants to meet you, Duchess," Carolus said. "He says his name is Inspector Dormouse. He is head of the…"

"…Department of Insanity," Margaret said. "What does he want?"

"He says he has critical information that you need to know."

"What kind of information?"

"Carter Pillar."

"What about him?"

"The Inspector says he's discovered something about him."

"Something that I don't know?"

"He says he knows who the Pillar really is."

"Nonsense." Margaret gently rubbed her son's picture. "I know all I need to know about the Pillar; all the way back since the days in Wonderland."

Carolus took his time in saying, "Do you know why he killed the twelve men, though?"

Margaret put her son's picture aside. "He did it so he could plead insanity and be admitted to the Radcliffe Asylum to mentor Alice."

"Don't you think he could've found easier ways to sneak into the asylum?"

"Of course. He could've worn a tutu, stood in Parliament Square, and cursed the Queen of England," she said. "But being the Pillar, he had to act larger than life and do crazy things, so he killed twelve people, claiming the *Alice Underground* book drove him crazy."

"That's not what Inspector Dormouse said."

"Whatever he said, I wouldn't trust a man who is asleep half of the time."

"Maybe that's why he sees things clearer."

"Meaning?"

"We're always awake. Always alert. Always thinking. Too much information could be the reason why we overlook a few details."

"Don't lecture me, Carolus. Don't act like you're a real person. You're merely a man's shadow. What did Dormouse say?"

"He wants to meet first, but he says he knows the twelve people the Pillar killed weren't chosen haphazardly. They all actually have one thing in common."

"Which is?"

"He wouldn't tell. That's why he wants to…"

"All right." Margaret sighed. "Make him pay me a visit at the office today. I'd love to see the Queen chop off his head for wasting my time."

"That'd put him into an eternal sleep." Carolus chortled. "And, ah, I forgot. There's one other thing."

"What now?"

"A madman by the name of the Chessmaster is holding the world's leaders hostage and is threatening to kill them all at that world charity event."

"Hostages? How is that possible? Why would someone do that?"

"Not only hostages, but he also killed the Pope's representative in a weird game of chess."

Margaret went silent. She felt a lump in her throat. She should have been the first to know, but she was too occupied with planning to save her son.

The event had been endorsed by the top five countries in the world. A global chess game to raise money. The Queen of Hearts had sent her new prime minister puppet, Mr. Paperwhite, to attend it.

"Duchess?" Carolus' voice crackled in the speaker.

"Forget about Dormouse," she said. "Call my staff for an emergency meeting. Until then, I want to know everything about this Chessmaster."

Chapter 4

Mr. Jay's limousine, Oxford

The Red pulls me out of the window. I find myself floating in the air, clinging to his wrist, baffled by the way he is balancing himself atop the limousine like a surfing master.

"Take her to Mr. Jay and make sure to evade the Pillar," the woman demands from the limousine below.

The Red doesn't answer her, and pulls me farther up, jumping over the car, down onto the pavement of whatever city I'm in now.

Now safe, I kick the Red, aiming for his groin, but miss due to his seamless maneuver with his waist. He swivels me as if in a dance, and we end up chest to chest. I try kicking with my knees, but his grip on my waist never falters.

"Let go of me," I scream like a little girl, which I don't like at all. "Don't you know who I am? I am Alice Wonder, Mary Ann, Black Chess's most precious."

The Red still doesn't speak, and I can't see his face under the hood.

"Is that you, Pillar?" I squint.

No response.

It's not the Pillar. He didn't come to save me like the woman suggested. It seems like Black Chess sent their best Red this time, making sure I end up meeting Mr. Jay.

Tons of police cars suddenly arrive. They stop before us, wheels screeching, doors opening, and someone is shouting in the speakers.

"Drop your gun!" A chubby police officer jumps out of the car, pointing his gun at the Red.

But, of course, the man gripping me neither flinches nor responds.

"Drop your gun or I will shoot!"

"He doesn't have a gun!" My voice is barely louder than a whisper as the Red's tight hands are pressed on my chest. "Just arrest him."

"I can't arrest him unless he chooses not to drop his gun," the chubby police officer says.

"Didn't you just hear me?" I snap. "He doesn't have a gun."

"Then we can't arrest him," the officer says. "We only arrest criminals who refuse to drop their guns."

I roll my eyes, confused. "But it's your responsibility to save me."

"Is it?" He scratches his head.

I squint against the ridiculousness of his question. "Of course it is. He is kidnapping me!"

"He is?" He tilts his head toward his fellow officer, a lanky young man. "Does that man in the red robe look like he is kidnapping this lady?"

The lanky officer holds on to his belt instead of his gun so his trousers won't slip down. "Hmm," he says. "They could as well be embracing. I mean, they're standing chest to chest. The man in the red robe seems fond of her."

"Lovers, you think?" the chubby officer says.

I am still not registering the stupidity of the conversation.

"Must be lovers," the lanky officer says. "Is it Valentine's Day yet?"

"It's not bloody Valentine's Day, you fool," the chubby one says. "They must be shooting a movie."

"What the heck are you talking about?" I shout. "This man just kidnapped me from the limo behind me."

"I don't have proof of this. I'm sorry," the chubby officer says. "I mean, I'm not sure he is kidnapping you." He lowers his gun. "I'm not even sure why I am here." He turns and asks his men, "Does anyone know why we're here?"

"You told us to follow you here," an officer responds.

"Hmm." The chubby officer turns and faces me, then rubs his chin. "I seem to have forgotten."

"It's really puzzling." The lanky one nods. "It's almost like a movie scene. Something wrong happens and the police arrive on the spot."

"I've never understood that." The chubby one turns and converses with his friend. "I mean really, who calls the police in those movies? The director of the movie?"

"Are you out of your mind?" I shout, unable to fathom the situation.

"Gotcha!" The lanky one pulls his trousers up to his chest, then snickers.

"She really took the bait." The chubby one laughs at me.

"What the heck is going on?" I ask.

Out of nowhere, tens of Reds jump out of the cars. Next to them, the police officers take off their uniforms, revealing Reds robes underneath.

"That was fun, wasn't it?" The chubby man jumps up and high-fives the lanky one, who drops his trousers but catches them halfway down. "Give her to us," he says to the silent Red gripping me. "You've done a good job and we've had some fun. Mr. Jay is waiting for her."

Feeling humiliated, I assume the Red behind me is going to hand me to them. But instead, still just as silent, he pulls out a sword and flashes it toward them, chopping off their heads one by one.

At first he does it while he is still gripping me with the other hand. It's like a dance of death. A ballet of incomprehensible killing techniques. The Red is a master who is killing his own people with a fluency I have never seen before. I glimpse a couple of None Fu techniques among his plethora of unbelievable moves.

But before I witness the end of the massacre, I bump my head on the back of his sword and fall unconscious, not knowing what the hell just happened.

Chapter 5

Buckingham Palace, Queen's garden

The Queen of Hearts had her men lined up on the vast chessboard, which she had planted at the bed of her garden. The chess tiles were white squares of grass amidst black squares of black roses. Her gardener had told her that the white plants were special winter lilies, which had been exclusively imported from Siberia. When she'd asked the name of the black roses, she was shocked with the response. At first she'd thought they were painted black roses, but her gardener had told her they weren't. They were called Black Shit Roses, and they only grew in her royal garden.

But that was of no concern to her now. All she wanted was to treat herself with a human-sized chess game, using her less-than-smart guards as chess pieces. It seemed like a fascinating idea, using humans for chess. Because, after all, a politician's best talent was to do so.

"They're ready, my Queen," said the chubby boy with the ice cream in his hand. Margaret's boy, whom the Queen took care of now, teaching him the science of all bonkers and evil. "Red guards against white guards. I've lined them up like a chessboard."

"Brilliant, Humpty Dumpty." The Queen called him by his Wonderland name, which Margaret had hated all along. "Have you taught them how the game is played?"

"Of course," Humpty chirped with lips smeared with ice cream. "You tell them the move you have in mind, and they obey without questioning you, as if they weren't human."

"Just like in real life." The Queen smiled. "My government tells people what to do and they just do it. Sometimes we make them think this is what they want to do, so they do it without knowing it's what we want them to do, but that's another story. So what happens if one of my chess pieces decides to disobey me?"

"They get their head chopped off, my Queen?" Humpty tilted his head, which was so heavy, he almost lost balance and fell.

"Exactly." She patted his bloated face with her chubby hands. "And please don't call me 'my Queen.'"

"Really? What should I call you?"

"Call me 'Mum.'"

Humpty looked reluctant, but then she pushed the fat cone of ice cream down his throat and he didn't care anymore, as long as he was fed.

"But I have a question, Mum," he said through blotchy lips. "Who are you playing against?"

"My dogs." She pointed at them panting with excitement on the other side of the board.

"Dogs?" one of the guards standing on the chessboard said.

"Yes, dogs." The Queen stood straight. "Haven't you seen a queen play chess with her dogs before?"

"But how are we supposed to understand what the dog wants us to do?"

"Just like you understand me. I talk. They woof. Not much of a difference," she said.

"Woof?" the guard, whose position was a pawn on the chessboard, said.

"I'll show you." She stood by the side of the board and ordered her dogs to kick-start the game.

The dogs didn't get it at first, still panting with excitement, probably waiting for their Brazilian nuts.

"Come on, sweeties," the Queen said. "Make your move."

"Woof. Woof," barked the dog in front, staring right at the reluctant guard.

"See?" The Queen waved both hands sideways. "Woof. Woof."

"So?" The guard grimaced.

"So follow the orders and make the move." She began to tense and become annoyed.

"Woof. Woof." Humpty laughed at the guard.

"Don't interfere, Humpty. Let Mum take care of this," the Queen said. "You better stick to 'lick, lick.'"

The dog barked again.

"I don't know what I should do," the guard said.

"What does a pawn do in chess?" the Queen asked.

"They either advance or move diagonally," the guard answered.

"Elaborate," she said, chin up.

"The pawn moves ahead, only if there is free space. Diagonally if they eat another chess piece."

"Do you see anything you can eat diagonally?"

"No, my Queen."

"So the dog can only order you to move forward, right?"

The guard shrugged. "Yes, my Queen."

"And how many squares does a pawn advance in the beginning of a chess game?" The Queen flashed a smug smile.

"Two squares, my Queen."

"And what did my genius dog say?"

"Woof. Woof."

"Two woofs, right? Two square moves for a pawn. I rest my case." She rested her hands on her hips and sighed.

The guard walked two squares ahead.

"Bravo!" She clapped at her dogs, as they drooled with excitement.

"But what if the dogs want me to move diagonally?" the guard asked.

"You still don't get it?" The Queen jumped in her place. "The dog will woof once and you will have someone to eat diagonally."

"I understand, my Queen." The guard was already sweating, partially confused, partially humiliated, and partially thinking he'd gone mad.

"So let's start the game." The Queen clapped with enthusiasm. "Woof! Woof!"

"What does it mean now?" The guard looked confused.

"Nah, that's not for you," she said. "This is for the guard next to you, so he can chop off your head for being stupid, unable to understand the clear and precise and unmistakable language of dogs."

In an instant, the guard's head was chopped off, blood spilling on the grass.

Humpty laughed harder, licking his ice cream.

"From now on, I will not say 'off with their heads' anymore," the Queen announced to her guards. "I will say 'woof woof!'"

It was in that instant when Humpty's big and stocky head was chopped off by the guard standing next to him.

"What did you do, you fool?" the Queen screamed.

"You said woof, woof," the guard said.

And then another guard's head was chopped off.

The dogs began to bark. Woof. Woof.

In a few seconds everyone's head in the garden had been chopped off, each rolling across the life-sized chessboard.

The Queen stood pouting and staring at the massacre in her garden, the dogs staring back at her. "What can I say?" she told them. "Humans are definitely woof, woof."

Chapter 6

Alice Wonder, somewhere in a dark room

When I wake up, I am too weary to fully open my eyes. The floor underneath me is cold and hard, and the ceiling, if there is any, seems so far away I can't see it.

In the back of my head, there is a continuous buzzing, a sharp, needlelike pain that won't stop. I reach back to touch it and instantly remember the strange incidents in the limousine, and the mysterious Red who seemed to have kidnapped me, but then rescued me as well.

My eyelids hurt when I squint and look sideways to inspect the rest of wherever I am. All I see is blurry darkness, pierced by a slant of yellow light, slithering diagonally from a top window. I think I am in some kind of a dungeon.

Slowly I prop myself up on all fours, hardly finding the strength to stand up. There is a tray of food next to me. A sandwich, a glass of water, and next to them is something I didn't expect. My precious Tiger Lily.

I reach for it instantly, remembering my future children—though I'm not comfortable with the memory of my future husband, whom I don't know anything about. I hug my Tiger Lily, almost sure it won't spit at me and call me insane anymore. As far as I know, I am not insane. I am only dealing with an insane world.

Still, I must have been insane once, with all the Lullaby pills, what happened in the circus, and whatever reason that turned me into the Bad Alice in the past.

It only takes a minute for my eyes to adjust to the semidarkness, and realize there is someone standing before me. The silent Red who saved me.

"Who are you?" I say, holding tighter to my Tiger Lily and crawling back against the wall.

He says nothing. Doesn't even move or make a sound.

"Listen," I say. "You will have to talk to me and explain who you are, or I will hurt you. You know who I am, right?" I am well aware of the nonsense I am speaking. I can't hurt him. He is too strong and I actually owe him for saving me from the rest of the Reds. Only I need to know what he wants with me.

The answer comes in the shape of a yellow note. A sticky one, which he writes on with a red pencil then hands to me. I take it, noticing it's of the same material as the note with the Pillar's Wonder written upon it. The one that is buried at the bottom of Tiger Lily's pot, which I am now holding.

I read the note: *You're a horrible Bad Alice. I thought you'd be able to fight me back.*

"What the heck?" I chortle.

He passes me another note. I take it and read it: *Heck is too American for a British girl that inspired Lewis Carroll. But you're forgiven, since you have no idea who you really are yet.*

I am not sure if this is supposed to be a joke, but I can sense the Red isn't here to harm me. "Why did you save me?"

Another note: *Consider me your guardian angel.*

"I don't need a guardian," I say. "And I am not sure angels are on my side at this time."

Note says: *You talk too much.*

I say, "As if you talk at all."

Note says: *I made a choice not to. You, on the other hand, do talk, so use your mind and focus, or blabbing will kill you.* Then he writes something that makes me chuckle. *Too much yappening, not enough happening.*

"And you make fun of me speaking in American terms?" I retort. "What you just said isn't even English."

A note: *It's better than English. It's nonsense.*

I don't reply, watching him churn out another note. This one says: *We may have started on the wrong note. Let's start all over again.*

"That sounds better," I say. "Where do you want to start?"

A note: *Let's begin with introductions. You can call me Dude.*

"Nice to meet you, Dude—I guess." I struggle and stand up on my feet, and stretch out a hand.

He doesn't shake it, but tucks another note in it: *Time is running out. You have to get ready for your next mission.*

"You're giving me orders now?" I ask.

A note: *Yes. The world is counting on you to save them from the Chessmaster.*

Chapter 7

The Dude tells me all about the Chessmaster, the best chess player in history, who's just gone mad and killed the Pope's representative while entrapping the world's leaders in an auditorium in Russia.

Then he makes me watch the news covering the catastrophe.

"But they don't mention why he is doing this," I say.

No one knows yet. He didn't say.

"Does the Chessmaster have a name?"

No one's sure. He has been concealing his identity for years, even when winning chess championships each year. Some say his real name is Vozchik Stolb.

"Sounds like a Russian name."

Who cares? You just need to stop him.

"So he is not a Wonderland Monster," I say. "You understand I only catch Wonderland Monsters, right?"

That's exactly why I am here, giving you orders, and not the Pillar.

"You know about the Pillar? Who are you?"

I'm the Dude. I told you that. I am here to teach you that you don't only save lives by beating Wonderland Monsters. You're obliged to save anyone harming humans in this world.

"And why would I do that?"

Because you have a responsibility to repent for the things you've done in the past.

"Seriously." I glare at his hollow face under the hood. "Who are you?"

I'll answer you when you know who you are.

"I know who I am, smartarse."

Really? Bad Alice? Good Alice? Insane? Sane? Alice? Mary Ann? Orphan? Family? You don't have the slightest idea.

I shrug. It's hard to argue with the only person bothering to save my life, other than the Pillar.

We may not have time, since the Chessmaster is playing the game with the world's leaders right now, and they are very bad at chess. Soon, another world leader will die—it's already a mess at the Vatican. People are angry and worried for the Pope's life.

"I thought it was the Pope's representative who died."

The Pope was forced to play the game after his representative died. He is present in Russia, endorsing the charity event. He happens to have no idea how to play chess. Now the Chessmaster is forcing him to play. Either win or die.

"This is getting serious." I rub my chin. "Do you happen to know where the Pillar is?"

I thought you'd never ask. Then he writes down an address. *I will drive you there, but then you'll not see me again. My role ends here.*

I don't know why I feel a bit lost, realizing I want to see this mysterious Red again. But it seems weird to vocalize my interest in him. I am not even sure I can fully trust him, so I take the note and we descend the stairs of the abandoned building we're in. Out to the streets, I immediately recognize the city of London.

The Red shows me to a Corvette in a vacant back street and opens the door for me.

"Must be rich," I mumble, sitting.

I borrowed it from a rich guy.

"You mean you stole it from a rich guy." I pull on the seatbelt.

He doesn't write a note and starts the engine.

"I'm really worried about the Pope," I comment, thinking about who this Chessmaster may be, and if he will end up being a Wonderland Monster. "You said the Chessmaster forced him to play and he has no clue how to play chess. What's the Pope doing now?"

He writes a note with one hand while driving with the other. *The Pope made his first move. It's a very common move in the Vatican when facing crisis.*

"Which is?"

A note with a smiley face: *Praying.*

Chapter 8

Buckingham Palace, Queen's garden.

The Queen watched her doctors trying to put Humpty Dumpty's head back on. They struggled with it. The boy's head was much heavier and bigger than most children his age. It was also a horrendous operation knitting it back.

"So he's going to live?" the Queen asked, chin up, hands behind her back, wearing rabbit flip-flops for a change.

"It's too soon to tell," the doctor said. "We're knitting the head back on. The rest needs divine intervention."

"What's divine intervention?"

"It's when you need God to intervene and save someone."

"Never heard of that," the Queen said, rubbing her chin.

"It's like when God lets people live while he decides others will die."

"Ah." She clicked thumb and forefinger. "You mean like when I chop off heads or don't chop off heads. I decide who lives and who dies."

The doctor shrugged, not sure if he should object or explain things further. He certainly could get his head chopped off if he spoke.

"Anyhoo," she said, smiling.

"Anyhoo?" the doctor asked.

"It's a hip word I heard the kids say," she said. "I like it. Nonsensical, and I like how you have to ball up your lips in the end like you're going to kiss someone. Any-*hoooo*."

"Whatever you say, my Queen."

"So like I said: Anyhoo, I think my Humpty will live. It happened to him before in Wonderland. He'd fallen off a wall and splashed open like an Easter egg. Lewis wrote a rhyme about it."

"And he still lived?"

"Yes. Became a little dumber, though. He is like an egg. You can certainly glue its shell, but you can't squeeze the yolk back in."

"I don't think we can afford him becoming any dumber," the doctor said, staring at Humpty balled up on the table.

"What's wrong with dumb?" she demanded. "I love dumb people. Now get your *dumb* arse out of my chamber before I chop it off." She stopped in her tracks, a forefinger pressed to her lips. "Did I just say I love your arse in the last sentence?"

The doctor suppressed a laugh and hurried toward the door.

"Wait," she said. "Margaret will want to see me because of this Chessmaster situation. I don't want her to see her kid like this or she will give me a hard time, so tell her I am busy."

"Busy?" the doctor said. "Doing what?"

"I am the Queen, dammit! I can be busy playing with my big toe if I want to. Get out!"

Then she patted the poor kid while staring at the massacre in the garden. It was mesmerizing staring at the dead guards who'd just killed each other over a woof, woof.

But she had no time for lamenting. She picked up the phone and dialed a fourteen-digit number.

"Mr. Jay," she said. "I assume you heard about the Chessmaster."

"I did, and I don't like it." The answer came in low tones from the phone.

"Let me guess. You don't like it because we don't know who he really is?"

"That's exactly it. I've never heard of a Chessmaster in Wonderland. True, Lewis had been obsessed with chess after visiting Russia, where he invented the famous *zashchishchaiushchikhsya* None Fu move, but he never revealed the Chessmaster's identity."

"Not even in *Alice Through the Looking Glass*?"

"I'm sure not."

"So, all we know is that the Chessmaster knows what the Six Keys are for?"

"That's all Lewis mentioned in his diaries, but I'm starting to doubt that. I'm not sure."

"If I may ask, sir," the Queen said, "aren't you supposed to know what the keys are for?"

"Of course I do—so do you and most of those interested in the Wonderland Wars."

"So why is the Chessmaster important? We can nuke him like we did Hiroshima when you advised the Americans to do so, and get rid of him. I know we'd lose the world leaders, but I've already planted their substitutes of my madmen all over the world. We could rule the world tomorrow afternoon."

"It's not about knowing what the keys' ultimate purpose is—we both know what that is. The problem is what do they open to get to our ultimate purpose."

"Ah." The Queen scratched her head. "So even knowing their location now isn't enough, because we don't know where to stick them."

"Stick them, yes." Mr. Jay sounded irritated with her. "Call me when you know something. I have other concerns at the moment."

"Really?"

"Someone kidnapped Alice on her way to my castle, and I need to know who he is, then get her back."

Chapter 9

Lifespan Hospice, London

After the Dude drives me to the Pillar's location, he guns the Corvette into the streets and disappears, leaving me with my mouth agape, staring at the hospice where I am supposed to find the Pillar.

I enter, not sure what the Pillar is doing here, so I ask the receptionist about him.

"Oh, Mr. Pillar," she cheers "Such a charming man. He is in Ward Six."

"Charming indeed," I mumble, a little envious of everyone finding him so, not pointing out that he is utterly bonkers—and a serial killer.

Inside, I try to smile at everyone I pass by in the rooms. I mean what consolation can you give to a dying person, though I totally respect the work done here.

Then there I find him, in Ward Six. He is standing on top of a patient's bed, dancing with his cane up in the air and the hookah in his other hand. I can't hear what he's saying, since I am behind glass. But I can surely see what the other patients are doing.

They are simply dancing as well, half of them smoking hookahs—and coughing ferociously afterward.

I rap on the glass but no one's paying attention. The Pillar's dance moves are imitated by each person in the room, all of them standing on their beds.

Pushing the glass door open, the first sound that attacks my ears is a well-known song, booming out of an eighties cassette player that most youngsters of my generation only see in old movies. The player is crackling with a badly equalized version of "Don't Fear the Reaper."

I call out for the Pillar, but still no one pays attention. Everyone is dancing and smoking as if they're reckless teenagers with no respect for what time does to us in this world. None of them look like they're dying soon, actually.

"Listen. Listen!" The Pillar waves at them. "We've danced enough."

"No!" They pout.

"Seriously." He coughs with beady eyes. "I need to tell you something."

"That you're handsome?" An old woman, who ripped her IV from her arm, giggles.

"Thank you, darling, but I already know that," he says. "What I want to tell you is a phrase, which I want you to repeat whenever you feel your time has come and that you're about to die."

The room falls silent. Even the song ends on its own.

"Don't worry," the Pillar tells them. "When death comes creeping up to your bed, under the sheets, telling you it's time, all you have to say is the following…"

The patients' eyes are all on him.

"You say, 'I will die when I say so,'" the Pillar says, and I feel embarrassed. The man must have smoked too much and now is only talking nonsense.

But the patients surprise me by loving it. They all start saying, "I'll die when I say so!"

Rolling my eyes, I pull at the Pillar's trousers while he is standing on the bed. He kicks me off, grunting. "What do you want? Get out of here."

"Seriously?" I say. "This Chessmaster is threatening to kill the leaders of the world and you're playing games with these poor people?"

"He isn't fooling us." The old woman glares at me. "Carter is one of us. He knows how we feel."

I shrug, speechless, unable to comment. What does she mean? Is the Pillar dying?

"Wait outside, Alice," the Pillar says. "You have no idea what's going on."

Chapter 10

Outside the Lifespan Hospice, London

"What was that all about?" I ask the Pillar, once he walks outside on the pavement.

"What?" He shakes his shoulders, pacing ahead.

"You're deluding people by promising them they can stand in the face of death. I find it unethical."

"Unethical?" He rolls his eyes. "I'm sure death is pretty unethical, too."

"What's that supposed to mean?"

"Fight unethical with unethical," he tells me. "Or better, fight death with nonsense. Laugh at it. I'm pretty sure Einstein said that."

"I'm sure he didn't. And what did the woman mean by saying you're one of them?"

"Forget about it, Alice."

"I want to know." I grab his arm, stopping him. "Are you dying?"

The Pillar shoots me a flat stare. It's the one he uses to conceal a big secret. I know him well enough to tell by now.

"Pillar," I say gently. "If you're dying, you have to tell me. Is it that skin issue you have?"

"Someone is going to kill me." He knocks his cane once on the ground, his face strangely unreadable.

"Are you psychic now, knowing someone is going to kill you?"

"I've seen it in the future." His chin is up, and he's avoiding my eyes.

The realization strikes me hard. "Is that why you were the same age when we time-traveled in the future? Because you weren't supposed to be there?" I cup my hands on my mouth. God, the Pillar will be dead fourteen years from now.

"I saw my grave, Alice."

"And it said you were killed, not a normal death?"

The Pillar nods, though I still feel he isn't telling me the whole truth.

"So you feel like you basically belong in the hospice, waiting for your death? That's not like you."

His flat expression lasts a whole minute, torturing me with his silence, as I fail to read his mind. It ends with him walking away toward the street.

"Where are you going?"

The Pillar doesn't answer, but stops at a café a little later. I stop next to him, watching the café's TV broadcasting the latest news about the incident in Russia. The host comments on the Pope's bad moves in the game and that he may be the next to die. The screen shows the world leaders sweating at their chessboards, most of them having played two moves out of the seven. Most of them have also sipped that poison that might eventually kill them.

"How can he possibly play with hundred and thirty people at once?" I ask.

"It should be easy for a man who played chess with God and won." The Pillar drags on his pipe.

"You don't really believe that."

"It's a great marketing scheme, instilling fear in everyone. It works. I don't have to believe it." The Pillar nears the TV. "Nice handlebar mustache, and look at that armor he is wearing."

"He is a madman who needs a psychiatrist," I comment.

"Or a fashion designer," the Pillar says. "I find it humiliating that the world is threatened by a man so out of fashion that he's still wearing armor."

"Do you know him? Is he a Wonderlander?"

"I'm not sure. I've certainly never met him before."

"He looks very much like Wonderlanders," I say. "Eccentric, mad, and evil."

"You've just described every politician on TV."

"This chess game strikes me as a Wonderland theme." I stare the Pillar in the eyes. "Like the chessboard of life in the Vatican."

"Are you implying something?"

"I think you know who he is and aren't telling me."

"Usually I am, but not this time."

I try to believe him but can't. "So why is the Chessmaster doing this?"

It's exactly this instant when the Chessmaster approaches the camera and begins to talk.

"I will be brief," he says. "Before I reveal my intentions and demands, I need to make sure only those who are qualified to meet my needs apply."

We all watch him pull each side of his handlebar mustache after every couple of words.

"Listen carefully," the Chessmaster continues. "Because you have no idea who I am. I mean, I am so scary that I sometimes prefer not to remind myself who I am."

"You think he could be the mad barber on Cherry Lane Road, who's responsible for half of the male Brits being bald?" the Pillar comments, but everyone in the café shushes him.

"In order to let your world leaders live, I need you to bring me something," the Chessmaster says in his Russian accent. It makes him sound both funny and intimidating, which puzzles me. "I want you to find something called 'Carroll's Knight.'"

Everyone in the café starts to murmur and speculate. I look at the Pillar for answers.

"Carroll's Knight." He drags from his pipe. "Sound's interesting."

"Don't bother trying to figure out what it is," the Chessmaster says. "Only those who already know will understand."

"I guess my work is done." The Pillar is on his way out of the café. "Because I don't know what Carroll's Knight is."

"Wait," I say. "The Chessmaster must be a Wonderland Monster. Carroll's Knight sounds Wonderland related."

"To get what I want, I will ask you to solve the following puzzle," the Chessmaster says. The Pillar stops at the door. I guess he can't resist puzzles. "If you are the few who are capable of getting what I want, you should be able to answer the following question. It's a puzzle, the answer to which leads to a place."

Everyone is listening.

"The puzzle is: Where is Miss Croatia 1454?"

Chapter 11

The streets of London

The Cheshire now possessed a politician's body. A middle-aged minister in an ironed suit and tie. After ordering people left and right, he sat back in his comfortable chair and glanced at the rainy London through his office window.

It wasn't like the Cheshire hadn't possessed politicians before. Only this time he made sure not to let his persona overcome that of the politician. Instead, he let the man's mind seep through, so the Cheshire could read it all.

It wasn't surprising how the politician didn't give a damn about the world's turmoil at the moment. The man rocked in his chair, lit a cigar, and started thinking about how he could benefit from the crisis of the Chessmaster holding the world's leaders hostage.

His thoughts were like this: *Would the American dollar rise or decline in such times? Never mind the British pound. It may be as strong as a rock, but it means nothing in the world's economy. Should I be investing in certain things now? Should I start planning to take the prime minister's place?*

In short, the politician was a scumbag, and the Cheshire was far from surprised. It was what he'd always expected from humans, though he'd begun mildly sympathizing with humanity, especially since he'd time-traveled to the future and possessed Jack's soul.

Of course, it baffled him how he partially remembered that journey when he shouldn't know anything about it. He couldn't explain it, and he didn't remember much anyways.

All he remembered was that fuzzy feeling in his chest toward Alice, which were Jack's feelings, of course.

But the Cheshire felt a bit changed since then. Not that he had converted to loving humans—the politician he was possessing made sure of that—but he was confused.

Part of the Cheshire's confusion was that he still didn't belong to a body or identity. It seemed like it was time he stuck to one person and lived their life. But who?

He picked up the remote and turned on the TV.

There was a show about cats, where a woman loved them and fed them and took care of them. All the cats looked really well groomed, too cute, too loving.

"Disgusting," the Cheshire said, and turned over the channel, wondering how much they paid those cats to act like they enjoyed the company of humans.

As he flipped through channels, he suddenly remembered that at some point he'd possessed the knowledge of the whereabouts of the Six Impossible Keys, but had forgotten them when he returned to the present again.

"Dang!" he said in the politician's voice.

He stopped at the channel that broadcast the Chessmaster in Russia and laid the remote on the table.

The Cheshire knew a few secrets about the Chessmaster. He even had an idea why he might be killing the world's leaders. A few secrets the Cheshire preferred to keep to himself.

The one thing he didn't know, that puzzled the purrs and furs out of him, was what, or where, Miss Croatia 1454 was.

Chapter 12

On the train, somewhere in Europe

I'm fidgeting in the seat next to the Pillar and slightly rocking to the train's movement. He doesn't pay attention to any of my questions, but stares at a paper he's discreetly pinned into the back of the woman sitting in front of him. She has bushy hair and probably hasn't washed it for some time, so she doesn't feel it.

"Aren't you going to tell me where we're going?" I ask him, disappointed that I've failed solving the puzzle.

"We booked two tickets for Croatia, didn't we?" he says, still staring at the paper, which reads, *Miss Croatia 1454.*

"I know, but this couldn't be so easy."

"The puzzle says Croatia, so it must be," he says. "All we need is to figure out what 1454 means. Could be an address."

"You mean a street or house number? Come on, he said only a few people will be able to solve it. That doesn't sound like a puzzle designed for a few people to get."

"I agree, but I can't solve it. Let's stick with the Croatia idea. What do you think the numbers are?"

"Coordinates?"

"I checked. It's not."

I let out a sigh. Today seems to be the day of disappointments. Earlier, I couldn't defend myself against the Reds, and now I am clueless to this puzzle. "Are you sure this isn't a Wonderland puzzle? Something Lewis Carroll wrote in his book?"

"I am. Lewis only left England to travel to Russia. I doubt it if he'd ever known anything about Croatia."

"Not even the 1454 number?"

"Nah, but wait." The Pillar waves his gloved hands in the air. These are new gloves the woman at the hospice gave him with her phone number on the back.

"What is it?"

"1454 is a year."

"I thought of it, Googled it, but found nothing of importance."

"Not even in Croatia?"

"I don't think Croatia existed in 1454," I say, wondering if he is testing me. Usually he knows more, though today he strikes me a little off balance with his worrying about dying within fourteen years. I wonder about the real reason he visited the hospice. I wonder if there is still a part of what he saw in the future that he hasn't told me about. And I hope he isn't really dying, because I am not sure what I'd do without him.

The Pillar pulls out a marker pen and stretches his arm forward, then crosses the word *miss* out. Instead he writes, *Ms.*

"What difference does it make?"

"All the difference in the world." He looks like he's got something.

Then I get it. It only takes a minute to see it, and I am proud of myself. "It's an anagram."

"Indeed," he says. "The words 'Ms. Croatia' are meant to be shuffled and changed to give us another word."

"The Chessmaster is brilliant. In order to make sure very few can solve it, he made it harder by substituting 'Ms.' with 'Miss.'"

"I wouldn't say that," the Pillar comments. "He said Miss Croatia, never wrote it. So it was up to us to interpret it the way we want."

"But now that we know 'Ms. Croatia' is actually the word..." I am trying to figure it out without pen and paper.

"Marostica," the Pillar says. "I am beginning to think I've underestimated the Chessmaster."

"Marostica?" I Google it. "That's in Italy."

"Yes, it is." The Pillar pulls the paper back and the woman flinches, glaring back at him. The Pillar sticks out his tongue like a kid, making her feel uncomfortable, she looks back immediately.

"So the message is Marostica 1454?" I whisper to him. "What happened in 1454 in Marostica?"

"Something beautiful," the Pillar says, booking train tickets to Italy on his phone.

"Something beautiful?" I squint. "I doubt the Chessmaster is inviting us to something beautiful."

"Dear Alice, buckle up and take a deep breath," the Pillar says. "The Chessmaster might be some sort of Wonderlander after all."

"I'm not following."

"Let me put it this way: in the year 1454 in Marostica, Italy, the first chess game in the history of mankind was played. Something Lewis had been very fascinated with."

Chapter 13

Marostica, Italy

The train stops at Bassano del Grappa, the nearest railway station to Marostica. Most tourists take the buses, but the Pillar insists on taking a private taxi, so in case someone is tracking us we can see them in the mirror. Who knows what the Chessmaster really has on his mind?

The Pillar converses with the driver in Italian, but I don't understand what they're saying. All I know is that the driver seems pretty amused with the professor, and at some point it seems they're talking about national football teams.

Marostica itself is one exceptional town. I imagine Jack taking me here and us having a good time. But Jack is part of my past now. I shouldn't be thinking about him, even if I want to.

Since we don't know where we should be going in Marostica, the taxi driver starts giving us a little tour. He shows us a few landmarks and recommends a couple of restaurants. But none of that piques our interest. Not until he shows us two castles, one at the top of the hill above town, the other in the main square, Piazza Castello. It's the one in the square that piques our interest.

The square before the castle is one large chessboard laid out in paving stones. I am not making that up. It's true.

The view with the upper castle, Castello Superiore, behind it is enchanting. The lower castle, directly overlooking the chessboard, is Castello Inferiore, and it guards the main entrance through the town walls as well.

We stop and get out and the taxi driver refuses to take any money, which doesn't strike me as an Italian behavior. He shoots me a pitying glance then says in English, "I pray for you," before he guns away.

"What was that all about?" I ask the Pillar.

"I told the taxi driver you were an insane girl who still thinks that Wonderland exists," the Pillar says nonchalantly.

"Why?"

"It helped us get a free ride, didn't it?" He pulls my hand and shows me ahead. "Now let me tell you about this place." He points at the people gathered around the large chessboard. "The famous Chess Game, or as the Italians like to call it: *Partita a Scacchi di Marostica*."

"So this is where the Chessmaster wants us to obtain his Carroll's Knight?"

"It has to be. Right here, the first ever chess game in history took place." He points at the live chess pieces, men and women dressed as such, gathering, each upon a square and pretending to be bishops, pawns, rooks, knights, kings, and queens.

"Really?" I say. "I mean, I never thought the first chess game was ever traceable."

"You're right about that. Let's just say this is the first documented chess game in history, here in Marostica in 1454. There is no doubt this is where the Chessmaster wants us to be."

"The only question is why."

"I imagine we're about to find out," the Pillar says. "Usually there is a yearly festival in the memory of that game, in September of each year."

"It's not September, so why are people gathered and celebrating?"

"My assumption would be that it's been planned by the Chessmaster."

A woman wearing what looks like a rook's top on her head approaches us and asks for tickets. The Pillar talks her out of it. She smiles pityingly and tells me she is going to pray for me.

"You have to stop that," I tell him.

"It got us a free ticket, didn't it?" the Pillar says. "Besides, I'm only telling the truth. You're a mad girl who thinks Wonderland exists. The game we're about to see, accompanied by dancing and music, involves scores of costumed participants and human chess pieces."

"So this isn't really a chess game?"

"No such thing. They're reciting a traditional story of a local ruler with a beautiful daughter. She had two suitors, but rather than letting them fight a duel, the lord proposed a chess match, with the winner receiving her hand in marriage and the loser marrying her younger sister."

"So she didn't have a say in the matter of her marriage?"

"They're not called the Dark Ages for nothing," the Pillar says. "What strikes me as interesting, though, is the fact that the first documented chess game in history was about two men trying to win one woman's heart."

"Are you trying to sound sentimental?" I mock him.

"Nah, I'm trying to remind you of your similar situation. You still don't know who you'll end up with. Jack or the mysterious future husband, but anyways, let's…"

This is when the Chessmaster's plan starts to reveal itself.

A tall man dressed as a black knight in the game on the large chessboard acts like he is about to checkmate the white queen, but with a mallet in his hand, he threatens to knock off her head.

Chapter 14

I am about to run toward him and stop him, when the Pillar squeezes my hand, pointing at the armed men in the higher castle, all pointing their weapons at the crowd below, including us.

People panic in a rage of murmurs, unable to comprehend or object to the situation. None of us understands what's going on until a large screen nearby broadcasts the Chessmaster live on TV.

"So, I believe that two people have solved my puzzle." The Chessmaster rubs his handlebar mustache, staring too close at the camera. "And that's where the game begins."

"Who is broadcasting this?" someone asks, but no one answers due to their paralyzing fear.

The Chessmaster proceeds. "Whether you're watching this on TV or are actually in Marostica in Italy, you will get to see live footage of what's happening now. To put it simply, the man with the sword will chop the head of the woman in the queen's outfit if my next puzzle isn't solved. Anyone who interferes will be shot by my men in the higher castle. Any other interference by air or military, I will kill the next president." He looks sideways at the sweating leaders of the world, trying to figure their next move in the chess game that may save their lives. "I believe I've clearly explained myself."

"Did he mean us when he talked about the two people in Marostica?" I whisper to the Pillar.

The Chessmaster answers me instead. "Please step forward, Alice and Professor Pillar."

"It's just Pillar," he says pompously. "I've not used that title in some time."

"Don't try to sound smart," the Chessmaster says. "You have no idea who I am or what I can do."

"Why are you doing this?" I shout at the screen.

"Well, first of all, it's fun," the Chessmaster says. "My other reasons should stay concealed for the moment. Let's just say this will help you find Carroll's Knight for me. Let's start with my first question or this woman in the white queen's dress will die."

Neither the Pillar nor I say anything. We've seen too many lunatics and know they've usually planned everything in advance.

"Here is my first question," the Chessmaster begins. "What was Lewis Carroll going to call the *Alice in Wonderland* book when he first wrote it?"

I am about to tell him *Alice's Adventures Under Ground*, but the Pillar squeezes my arm again. "Too easy," he says. "I doubt it's the right answer."

"But it *is* the right answer," I insist. "You told me so."

"Just think about it, Alice. The man looks like a loon. He wouldn't give it away so easily."

I try to make sense out of the Pillar's words, but the sight of the man lowering his sword toward the woman in white scares me. I snap. "It's *Alice's Adventures Under Ground*!" I shout out.

The Chessmaster says nothing, but pulls on his handlebar mustache again. One rub to the left. One to the right. "Wrong!"

And suddenly we're back in the Dark Ages again. The man's sword chops off the woman's head instantly.

I shriek, watching her bloody head roll all over the chessboard, not knowing how my answer is wrong.

"Checkmate!" The Chessmaster roars with laughter in the microphones. "Want to play again?"

Chapter 15

It's hard to imagine the world's reaction to what just happened, not to mention those watching this on TV, probably among their children at home. As for us here in Marostica, we're in a dreadful state of fear, since it seems like the Chessmaster has eyes in the sky. He seems so invincible.

"I haven't heard the right answer yet," he announces on the screen. "Until I do, more heads are going to roll."

The man with the sword has approached the next woman on the board, the one wearing the uniform of a knight. She was already shivering as he came closer.

"You're a liar!" I tell the Chessmaster. "I know my last answer was right."

"No, it wasn't," the Pillar says, looking disappointed he didn't figure it out sooner. "Lewis Carroll had many choices for the title of what became *Alice in Wonderland.* He listed them on a single page in his diary, which can still be found in the archived papers in the Surrey History Centre in London."

"What?" I am totally mad at the Pillar. "Why didn't you say so earlier?"

"Because it's such trivial information that no one ever mentions it anymore."

The Chessmaster applauds the Pillar by clapping both sides of his mustache. "That partially answers my question. Now let's make it harder. There are four titles on that page." The Chessmaster neglects my comments.

"Only one of them counts, because Lewis actually sent it to the printing house before he changed his mind."

I turn back and face the Pillar. The woman's life is in his hands now, and I am sure I don't have enough time to Google it, if this is even the kind of info I can find on Google.

"That's easy." The Pillar shrugs, glancing at the poor woman. I think he isn't sure of the answer, but spits it out anyways. "*Alice's Hour in Elfland* was the original title."

"In Elfland?" I say.

"Right answer," the Chessmaster says. "Weird, but right."

"I'm assuming you won't let the woman go anyways." The Pillar steps forward, flashing his cane. I'm terrified at the thought.

"Well, you assumed right," the Chessmaster says. "May I ask why you assumed so?"

"Because you're a lunatic, that's part of it," the Pillar says. "And because you're not here to spill blood and institute chaos. You have a bigger plan in mind."

The Chessmaster smirks, brushing his mustache. "Next question."

"Let the woman go first," I demand.

"Don't bother, Alice," the Pillar says. "He won't stop until he gets what he wants, though I am not sure what that is."

People suppress their shrieks all around us. They stand frozen in their places, some of them eying the snipers in the high castle, some of them watching the man with the sword on the chessboard.

"Next question is," the Chessmaster says, "name three masterpieces written in the same era *Alice in Wonderland* came out."

"*David Copperfield* by Charles Dickens." The Pillar shoots his words faster than the speed of nonsense. *"The Water-Babies* by Charles Kingsley, and *Great Expectations*, also by Charles Dickens."

"That's impressive." The Chessmaster claps again. "Why so fast?"

"Because it's common knowledge that in spite of the three masterpieces being the world's most awaited novels in that era, it was *Alice in Wonderland* that topped the bestseller list," the Pillar says in one breath. "Now let the woman go."

The Chessmaster ignores the comment and shoots another question. "What was so special about Alice's character in the book?"

"That's a vague question," the Pillar says.

"Let me rephrase: What was a first about Alice's character in Lewis Carroll's book?" the Chessmaster says. "Something that hadn't been done earlier in literature."

The Pillar grimaces, searching for answers, but it's me who surprisingly knows. I don't know how. It could be part of my lost memories coming back, or something that has been buried in me for years that I had just forgotten about.

"She was..." I begin, realizing that what I am about to say puts so much weight on my shoulders if I am the Alice in the book. So much weight that I feel I am not really doing enough to save the world or stand up to the model Lewis made out of me.

"She was what?" The Chessmaster nears the screen, eyes glinting.

"She was the first female lead in children's literature, ever," I say. "Before her, children's books had only male heroes."

Chapter 16

My words don't seem to affect the crowd around me. They're nothing but the right answer to them, so the woman won't get her head chopped off like the last. But to me, they make me ashamed of myself. Lewis wrote about me as the first girl in a children's book to stand up to adults and speak her mind freely and criticize the mad society she—or he—lived in. And still, I let him down and turned into a Bad Alice at some point in my life.

"Magnificent," the Chessmaster says. "I am now sure it's you and your old caterpillar who can find Carroll's Knight." He doesn't explain why and says, "But first, I need to give you the first clue, and to do so, you need to answer a question you don't have an answer for."

"You mean you want to kill this woman anyways, like the one before?" I clench my fist. "Why is it important you kill them?"

"Life is a game of chess, Alice. One move at a time. With each move, doors either open or close for the next. Some of us are lucky to come upon several doors in a row. Pure luck, if you ask me. Some are doomed with a closed door after their first move," the Chessmaster says. "Now here is my last question, after which, if you answer it correctly, I will let the woman go—but then again, you don't know the answer, and the Pillar isn't allowed to contribute."

"I am ready," I say.

"No, you're not, but here it is: What was the color of the cover of the 1865 version of *Alice in Wonderland* book, published by Macmillan at the time?"

"What kind of question is that?"

"The kind that kills," he says. "Lewis Carroll insisted on that color, even though his publishers thought it would scare kids away."

I glance at the Pillar, who looks like he knows the answer, but if he tells me, the woman dies. I myself have no idea. A color that Lewis Carroll insisted on nearly two centuries ago? Why would his book's color matter? Should I just make a guess?

"I don't know the answer," I tell the Chessmaster.

"Then the woman will die. Thank you very much."

We all watch the man with the sword about to chop off her head, but an old man calls out from the crowd, "Stop!"

The man with the sword actually stops, and even the Chessmaster seems to be interested in the old man from his screen.

"Stop! Don't kill my wife." The old man steps ahead with both hands in the air. "I will tell you what you want to know." He is speaking to the Chessmaster."

The Pillar and I exchange glances.

"Do tell," the Chessmaster says. "Before it's too late."

"I will tell you how to get Carroll's Knight," the old man says, now hugging his wife, who was about to get her head chopped off.

"So this is what it's about?" the Pillar says. "This whole game was a threat to make whoever knew the secret about Carroll's Knight speak up before his loved one died. This was never about Alice and me, or the puzzles."

"Genius, isn't it?" The Chessmaster winks.

"Sick," I retort.

"I had my doubts if it was the first woman or the second," the Chessmaster elaborates. "Since no one came to save the first woman, it wasn't her. But the second is. And her husband knows the whereabouts of Carroll's Knight. The book's cover was red, by the way," he tells me. "The color of the Red Queen, but that's a whole other story. Now let's hear it from this old man who knows the secret to Carroll's Knight."

Chapter 17

The man's name is Father Williams, which is a name the Pillar squints at, and I don't know why.

I am surprised the man isn't Italian. In fact, he comes from a family of English noblemen who have been instructed to live in Marostica all these years, as keepers of the secret of Carroll's Knight.

"What secret?" I ask him.

"I will show you," says Father Williams, gripping a torch and guiding us into the hallways of the high castle, Castello Superiore. "Follow me."

The Chessmaster isn't watching us at this point. He orders his man with the sword and a few snipers to follow us, until we get him Carroll's Knight and bring it back to him. I am most curious about what's really going on here.

"So your family was instructed to keep a secret in this town?" I ask Father Williams. "Why? Who instructed you?"

"Lewis Carroll," Father Williams says reluctantly. "It's his *knight* you're looking for."

"You mean what the Chessmaster is looking for," the Pillar says. "And by 'knight' you mean what exactly?"

"I don't know," Father Williams says. "I only know of the place and have been denied looking upon the tomb where it is by my father."

"Tomb?" I shrug, the shadows from the torch reflecting on the wall and worrying me.

"It's where the knight is kept," Father Williams says.

"So it's a person," the Pillar says.

"Like I said, I don't know."

"Do you at least know why Lewis hid it here?" I ask.

Father Williams stops and stares into my eyes. "I am told it holds great evil."

"Oh, please." The Pillar rolls his eyes. "Great evil in a tomb. Is that some Hollywood movie again?"

"I can tell you're scared," Father Williams tells the Pillar.

"I'm not scared," the Pillar says, though I think he is. Maybe he is claustrophobic. The castle's hallways are a bit too narrow and slightly suffocating. "I just hate this whole thing about an item that holds evil and will unleash it onto the world if you reopen it. I mean, if Lewis knew it was so evil, why not destroy it?"

"Agreed." I nod at Father Williams.

"Funny, coming from people interested in a book where a girl gets taller when she eats a cake and shorter when she drinks a drink." Father Williams' logic starts to amuse me. "Do you want the knight or not? I'd prefer to go spend time with my wife than with you."

"Please forgive us," the Pillar says, then whispers something in his ear.

Father Williams looks sympathetically at me and says, "I pray for you."

I pinch the Pillar immediately, but then the door to the tomb opens before us. *Carroll's Knight* is carved on the wall behind it.

Chapter 18

The tomb is not like anything I expected. Its walls and floor are covered in black and white tiles, and there is a coffin in the middle. One side surprises me with two dead men, now skeletons, leaning on a chessboard.

"Thieves," Father Williams explains. "Some claim they're Tweedledum and Tweedledee, but I doubt it."

"Then who are they?" the Pillar asks.

"They tried to steal Carroll's Knight," says Father Williams.

"Why are they dead on the chessboard, then?" I ask.

"The tomb has a locking system. They were locked in and, by a Wonderlastic spell, they were forced to play chess, not until one wins, but until both died."

"You people have really misunderstood that chess thing," the Pillar says. "Anyone told you it's just a game?"

"It's not a game," Father Williams insists. "Chess is life. Move one piece, take a step in life. Move another, yet another step. Make a bad move, spend a couple of moves correcting it and paying the price. And by move, I mean a year of your life."

"I dropped out of elementary school, so don't go poetic on me." The Pillar chews on the words.

"I take it you can't play chess," Father Williams says.

"If you mean pulling hair for hours to make one move in a game so slow it'd make a turtle bored out of its mind, then the answer is no, I can't play chess."

"You have a lot to learn, Mr. Pillar," Father Williams says. "And you,

Alice?"

"Me?" I shrug. "I'm fresh out of an asylum. Doctors advised me I stay away from too much thinking."

The Pillar looks like he wants to crack a laugh, but he goes inspecting the coffin instead.

"Now that you're here, I'll leave you to open it," Father Williams says.

"Wait." I wave a hand. "Open it? I thought you knew how to open it."

"I don't. I am just the keeper of the secret."

The Pillar and I sigh. Not again.

"It's shut and locked, so don't try to push anything, it won't work. I've tried," Father Williams says. "The key to unlocking it is in the groove in the middle of the coffin's lid."

I locate what he is talking about. The coffin is made of stone, and it's fixed to the floor. It doesn't seem to have a ledge or the slightest of openings. In the upper middle, probably upon the corpse's chest, is a small groove. It's neither circular nor diagonal. In fact, it's shapeless. It looks like three curving strokes that remind me of a palm tree with three branches, waving sideways in the wind.

"It's too small for someone's palm," the Pillar says. "Or we could have tried fitting one's fingers in the groove."

"We tried that too, even water, but it didn't work," Father Williams says.

"So there is not even a clue?" I ask.

"My father left me a clue, but I believe it's useless."

"Tell me about it," I say.

"Two words that hardly mean anything," Father Williams says.

"Hi ho?" the Pillar purses his lips. "Or hocus pocus?"

"No," Father Williams says. "It's 'her lock.'"

"Her lock?" The Pillar tilts his head. "What kind of clue is that? It's barely even proper English."

I give it a thought, but it's getting harder to concentrate with the noise that suddenly erupts outside.

"What's going on?" Father Williams asks the men escorting us.

"Someone burst through the door," one of his assistants says. "It's the Reds."

"If I had a smoke each time I bump into them…" the Pillar says.

"Don't worry," Father Williams says. "I'm sure the Chessmaster will stop them from harming us."

"No, he won't," I say. "He can't."

"Why so sure, Alice?" the Pillar says.

"Because the Reds don't work for the Chessmaster at the moment, but Mr. Jay. He sent a limo to drive me to his castle earlier and I escaped. They're here to finish what they started."

"So we're looking for a bloodbath in here," the Pillar says. "You have another way out of here, Father Williams?"

"None. We'll have to fight them."

"I'm not leaving this place," I tell the Pillar. "Not before I open the coffin."

A loud thud sounds outside. The Reds have already broken into the castle.

Chapter 19

The Inklings, Oxford

"Her lock?" the March Hare said, staring at the message Alice had managed to send to him by phone from Italy. He had stopped cleaning the bar's floor, and no matter how his ears perked up, he couldn't solve it. Sometimes the March didn't want to think too hard in case those who controlled the light bulb in his head read into his thoughts.

"So Alice is alive," Fabiola said from behind the bar, serving a couple of customers. "The Pillar only made us think she died."

The March didn't comment. Fabiola's quest to kill Alice had become redundant. He wondered if it was the whiskey she drank in the Inklings that messed with her head. Mental note, he thought: there is a reason nuns shouldn't drink whiskey or wear tattoos.

"Don't pretend you don't know, Jittery," Fabiola said.

"I am not pretending," he answered. "You should have known she was alive all along, if you'd switched on the TV and watched the news."

"I have," Fabiola said. "I just didn't want to think about it. My biggest priority now is to persuade the Mushroomers to be part of my army."

"Any luck, White Queen?" The March noticed a few customers' heads turning when he called Fabiola by her Wonderland name. But hey, who believed in Wonderland anyway?

"Tom Truckle is working on a serum that should bring sanity to the Mushroomers."

"Good luck with that." The March continued cleaning. "I doubt the pill-popping doctor can help anyone with their sanity."

"I hate it when I hear you talk like that," Fabiola said.

The March said nothing. To him, the war didn't mean anything. All he cared about was going back to Wonderland and never growing up again. He'd been reading *Peter Pan* lately, and the idea of never really growing up resonated with him even more. Adulthood sucked marshmallows.

"So tell me about the clue," Fabiola said. "Is Alice in trouble?"

"She is," the March said. "Reds again."

"Maybe they'll succeed in killing her this time."

In his mind, and though he respected Fabiola dearly, he wanted his broom to transform into a double-headed axe that he could roll in the air and immediately chop off her head with. The March loved Alice too much, and Fabiola was being unreasonable.

"It's a clue that should help her open a coffin with a groove in it," the March said. "It says 'her lock.' Do you happen to know about that?"

"Even if I did, I wouldn't tell you," she said. "But I'd assume it's a clue Lewis designed."

"Why so?"

"Because it's a Carrollian phrase. 'Her' refers to Alice. 'Lock' refers to…" Then she suddenly stopped.

"Lock refers to what?" The March was curious. "The lock on the coffin? A metaphor for the coffin being locked?"

Fabiola suddenly smiled. It was a devious smile. Very much unlike her. Sometimes the March wondered if she'd been possessed by the Cheshire. It would explain her sudden change. But the Cheshire couldn't possess Wonderlanders. Certainly not Fabiola.

"I think you know what the clue is," the March said.

"In fact, I do." Fabiola poured herself a drink, and then two free drinks for the customers at the bar. "But I am not telling. She won't be able to solve it anyways." She made a toast and gulped happily, leaving the March in pain, wondering what the world "lock" really meant.

Chapter 20

Castle Superiore, Marostica, Italy

Fighting the Reds in such a claustrophobic corridor proved to be overly bloody. Father Williams' men and the Chessmaster's snipers were dropping like flies outside the tomb. Alice could barely see them. She and the Pillar preferred to stay inside the room and try to unlock the coffin.

"I don't know how long before the Reds get into the tomb," Father Williams said. "The Chessmaster sent his men to attack them from behind, but it's only turning into a massacre, and I'm not sure who is going to win."

"We have very little time," I say.

"You mean before we die or solve the puzzle?" Father Williams chuckles worriedly.

"I am assuming the word 'her' means you, Alice." The Pillar is kneeling down to inspect the groove on the coffin again. "Lewis always referred to you as 'her,' let alone the fact that he always talked about you."

"So what does it mean?" I ask.

"It means the coffin is locked with your *lock*." The Pillar is only speculating. "I know it doesn't make sense."

"Or maybe it means that only I can unlock it," I offer.

"It's a probability, but how?" The Pillar grimaces at the sound of men dying outside.

"Hurry!" Father Williams says.

I stare at the coffin with no clue of how to unlock it.

"Who told you about this clue?" the Pillar asks Father Williams.

"My father."

"How so? Did he write it down for you or just say it?"

"Never wrote it down. The keepers of the secret always keep the clues in their minds."

"And I assume your father heard it from his father, and so on."

"I assume so," Father Williams says. "Why?"

"I am only trying to see if the clue is wrong, misinterpreted, or even misheard."

"I am sure it says 'her lock,'" Father Williams insists.

"What do you have in mind, Pillar?" I ask.

"I am not sure, but I have a feeling the word is alluding to something else, if not intentionally misheard. Lewis loved those kinds of misinterpretations."

"How so?"

"Like a game of Chinese whispers, when you whisper a word in someone's ears and it comes out something similar, but very different in meaning from the original."

"Like the word 'her' being 'hair,' maybe?" I am just going along, shoving the killing sounds outside behind me.

The Pillar's eyes widen, as if I've just discovered a way out of here.

"What is it?"

"'Hair' seems to be the solution." He stared at the groove in the coffin again. "The groove doesn't resemble bending palm trees, but a few hairies in the wind."

"That's ridiculous," Father Williams says.

"Even so, what does that mean?" I kneel beside the Pillar.

"It means that 'lock' doesn't mean 'lock' as in 'lock and key,'" he says.

"I'm not following." But then I realize I actually do. My mouth hangs open wide for a moment. "Lock as in a lock of hair."

"It's also a double entendre," he says. "A phrase or word open to two interpretations. 'Her lock' could mean her lock of hair. Or hair lock, which also means a lock of hair." The Pillar looks a bit dizzy, phrasing this and thinking about it. "Damn you, Lewis, for messing with my head. In all cases, the groove opens with a lock of your hair, Alice."

"My hair?" I ask. "How would you have come to this conclusion?"

"Because, my dear Alice," the Pillar says, "Lewis, as weird as he sometimes was, kept a lock of your hair as a bookmark in one of his diaries. A strange action, but a fact which scholars can't explain until today."

I am not sure about Lewis keeping a lock of my hair, but I don't sweat it. The Pillar, as resourceful as he always is, hands me a knife, and I cut a lock of my hair and set into the groove.

Instantly, we hear a click, and the coffin is ready to be opened.

"Hurry!" Father Williams urges us again. "The Reds are by the door."

The Pillar and I push the heavy coffin's lid open, and there it is, the thing that the Chessmaster calls Carroll's Knight. But it definitely is like nothing I ever imagined it would be.

Chapter 21

Carroll's Knight is so small I actually tuck it inside my pocket. "How is this thing in my pocket so important?" I ask the Pillar.

"I think I have an idea," he says. "But first we have to find a way out of here."

Through the slightly ajar door, I see the Reds winning outside.

"Soon they'll get in," the Pillar says. "We need to think fast."

"I can use my None Fu," I say.

"I doubt a nonsensical martial art would help in this narrow space," the Pillar says, then turns to face Father Williams. He shoots him a look like earlier. I am starting to believe the Pillar and Father Williams know each other. "How about you show us your talents in fighting the Reds, Father Williams?"

"Talents?" I ask. Father Williams is a bit old for knowing how to fight the Reds. He has bushy white hair, an arched back, and is pretty overweight, with a balloon belly.

"All right," Father Williams says. "You got me."

"So you are who I think you are," the Pillar says. "Just like in Lewis Carroll's poem."

"What poem?" I ask.

"Later, Alice," the Pillar says. "Let the old man help us out of here first."

Father Williams knuckles his fingers and takes a deep breath. "I haven't done this in a few years, so I may look a bit rusty."

"I'm sure rusty isn't that bad." The Pillar seems amused. "Why don't you start with your famous somersault?"

I am baffled, unable to fathom what's going on.

But Father Williams surprises me with an actual somersault, as if he were a teen ninja from an anime of ridiculous superheroes.

"Frabjous," the Pillar says, helping keep Father Williams stable on his feet. "Go get them!"

With a wide-open mouth, I watch Father Williams use his remarkable techniques, somersaulting, walking on walls, on hands, fighting with his bare hands, and kicking everyone's butt outside.

"What's going on?" I ask the Pillar.

"I will tell you on our way out." The Pillar elbows me and pulls me outside, where we start to descend the spiral stairs while Father Williams is kicking Reds left and right.

"How can he do that?" I ask.

"He is something, isn't he?" The Pillar enjoys the view of the fight from atop. "No wonder Carroll made him a keeper of secrets."

"Shouldn't we help him?" I say.

"Father Williams can take care of himself. Didn't you ever read Carroll's poem about him?"

"What poem?"

At this moment, things become extremely surreal. The Pillar recites Carroll's poem in a musical way that makes it sound like a soundtrack for Father Williams' killings left and right. It's a long poem, mentioned in few *Alice in Wonderland* copies. It describes an old man called Father Williams who has no worries about growing old. In fact, he eats like a young man, plays like a child, and plays sports as if he is a nineteen-year-old athlete. Part of the poem says:

"You are old," said the youth, "As I mentioned before,
And have grown most uncommonly fat [Father Williams];
Yet you turned a back-somersault in at the door—
Pray, what is the reason of that?"

It perfectly describes Father Williams, who is a miracle. Even the Chessmaster's men can hardly believe what's going on.

Once we reach the bottom of the stairs, the Pillar guides me to a side door, which I kick open. Right there before us is the large chessboard of Marostica, bordered by the Chessmaster's men in every direction.

I pull back my sleeves. "It's time to use my None Fu."

"No it's not," the Pillar tells me, but I can't see him. Where did he go? "If anyone really knows None Fu, it'd be Father Williams, not you."

"But he is still fighting the others by the stairs."

"That's why I am hoping you know how to ride a horse," the Pillar says. This time I locate him riding a horse, which the chess players originally used to resemble a knight on the large Marostica chessboard.

"I don't know how to ride horses," I say.

"Then hop on behind me," he says, and I do, clinging to him from the back. "It's about time we escape this place."

The Pillar rides away, only we're surprised when the horse doesn't run in straight lines, but in L-shapes, just like a knight is allowed to move on a chessboard.

Chapter 22

World Chess Championship, Moscow, Russia

Not for a moment did the Chessmaster hesitate with his moves. On the contrary, the world leaders took too much time. Part of it was squeezing their thoughts for a winning move, but most of it was stalling, in case Alice and the Pillar could find Carroll's Knight—whatever that was.

But the Chessmaster was losing patience and getting more furious by the minute, especially after Alice and the Pillar escaped with Carroll's Knight in their pocket.

The Chessmaster faced the camera and warned the world of the consequences that would occur if he didn't get what he wanted in a few hours. "This is a call to the world," he began. "Don't think I have no more rabbits under my hat. Killing your world leaders in a chess game is only the beginning. You don't want me to go further with my threats."

He walked with his hands behind his back, and the camera followed him. "Everyone in Italy is responsible for catching Alice and the Pillar. This or…" He stopped before the Italian president's table and grinned. "I will checkmate your president sooner than you think."

People gasped in the auditorium and the Italian president swallowed hard, thinking about his next move.

"Listen to me, people of this world." The Chessmaster faced the camera again, exercising his hobby of rubbing his mustache. "Like I said, you don't know who I am, and you probably don't want to," he said. "I'm not a Wonderland Monster. That would be an understatement. I'm your last and worst nightmare. Bring me Carroll's Knight or…trust me, I'll checkmate the world."

Chapter 23

Marostica, Italy

The Pillar stops atop an abandoned green hillside and we get off the mad horse.

"I need this to be mentioned in *Guinness World Records*," the Pillar says. "Having managed to escape with a horse that only runs in L-shapes."

"That was weird." I pat the horse. "You're a weird horse. Beautiful but weird."

I stare down below at Marostica, which is in a paranoid craze. The Chessmaster's men are still fighting the Reds, people are scared, but Father Williams is nowhere in sight.

On my phone, I watch the Chessmaster's speech and realize we're in so much trouble now.

"Almost everyone is looking for us," I tell the Pillar. "I think we should call Fabiola. She may help."

"Trust me, she won't help," the Pillar says. "She thinks you're the Bad Alice and wants to get rid of you." He raises a hand in the air. "And please, let's not discuss this now."

"You're right, we need to know what this is for." I pull out Carroll's Knight. "How can Carroll's Knight be a chess piece?"

"Not just any piece."

"What do you mean?"

"It's made from Carroll's bones."

Hearing that, I almost drop the piece. I think it's the fact that it's wrapped in transparent cellophane that makes me not do it. "Lewis's bones?"

"It's something that I've heard he did before he died," the Pillar explains. "He ordered Fabiola to carve little bits of his bones into chess pieces. No one's really sure what that was all about."

"Fabiola?"

"Don't even think about asking her. I doubt she will tell us."

"Because she thinks I'm the Bad Alice?"

"No, because Lewis kept a lot of secrets with her before he died."

"Why her? Why not me? I thought I was the closest to him. He wrote the book about me, not Fabiola."

"Alice." The Pillar eyes me. "You weren't the Good Alice in those days. You lost it, and turned bad. Lewis didn't really like you anymore."

I wonder how long I will be reminded of my bad past and feel guilty about it. "Then it's time for you to tell me what happened."

"What happened to what?"

"What made me become that Bad Alice?"

The Pillar's gaze freezes. I can't interpret it. Part of it seems like he is about to tell me. Part as if he is not. Mostly I get the feeling he can't tell me for reasons beyond him.

"You didn't ask me how I know the chess piece is Carroll's." He changes the subject, and somehow I don't mind.

"How did you?"

"It's a speculation, actually, because I was told that Carroll told Fabiola to scatter the chess pieces all over the world."

"I don't see the connection."

"If the Chessmaster, whoever he is, is looking for Carroll's Knight, and Father Williams was told to guard it all these years, then this must be it."

"Are you saying the Chessmaster is looking to find Carroll's chess pieces? Why?"

"I'm not sure, but one advantage we have is that he doesn't know where it is. This ballet of death he enjoyed at the chessboard was a trick to expose the keeper of secrets, Father Williams, into confessing the whereabouts of the piece we're holding."

"And it worked." I stare at the chess piece. "The one thing that I find odd is this piece in my hand not being a knight."

"You have a point. If it's called Carroll's Knight, why is it a white queen in your hand?"

"I think I know the answer," I say. "And it's going to drive the Chessmaster mad."

"I'm listening."

"I think the Chessmaster is after the knight but Carroll—or Fabiola— was too devious and scattered all the pieces around the world like you said. Now instead of Carroll's Knight, we have Carroll's White Queen."

"Do you think it may contain a clue to where the other pieces are?"

"Only one way to find out." I slowly pull out the wrapper and start inspecting the white queen for another clue.

Chapter 24

Director's office, Radcliffe Asylum, Oxford

"I need you to find the serum sooner," Fabiola told Tom Truckle. "I need to convert the Mushroomers into my army."

"It's a long process," Tom Truckle said, and popped down a couple of pills. "I am doing my best."

"Your best is not good enough. If Lewis made you create the asylum for the purpose of saving the Mushroomers, then you better be good for the job."

"You're not the only who cares about the war, Fabiola," Tom said. "Don't act like you know better."

"I know more than you even think I know!" She rapped her hand on his desk.

Tom swallowed a couple of more pills. "What the hell was I thinking, dragging myself into this Wonderland War?"

"You're a Wonderlander like all of us, so don't try to escape your responsibilities."

"I am a mere Mock Turtle. A useless and slow animal. I am soup at best," he lamented. "I'm so not important, Lewis only mentioned me in a single page in the whole book."

"I don't care," Fabiola said. "Find a serum. Bring those mad Mushroomers back to their senses. Make them fight the war they were destined to fight."

"Aye, aye, boss," Tom said. "All this aside, what about that Chessmaster?"

"What about him?"

"Who is he?"

"You don't want to know."

"That's not original, because that's what he said too."

Fabiola tapped her fingers on the table impatiently.

"If you tell me, I will expedite the serum's invention," Tom said.

Fabiola looked like she was going to choke him, but she seemed to need that serum badly. "All right. I will tell you. But I will kill you if you tell anyone else."

"Only me and my flamingo friend downstairs will know."

"Not even him, you understand?"

"I was joking. We all know now he is a spy for the Queen."

"Which makes me wonder why you haven't gotten rid of him yet."

"I thought he may be useful at some point."

"Whatever that means. I don't even want you to tell yourself what I am going to say to you."

"It's that secret?" Tom leaned back in his chair. Being closer to Fabiola was making him uncomfortable.

"It's that scary." She leaned forward, cornering him in a bad place. "The Chessmaster is…"

Fabiola suddenly stiffened in place. The veins in her neck stiffened too. Then she began shaking, hands on her stomach, and then vomited on Truckle's desk.

And before he knew it, the White Queen fell silently to her knees, hardly breathing, as if she was about to die.

Chapter 25

Marostica Mountains, Italy

The chess piece is a piece of art. It's small, but when I focus on it, I can totally admire the craftsmanship, though I am still unsettled by the fact that I am holding a piece of Carroll's bone.

"Let me inspect it." The Pillar pulls out a magnifying glass.

"Where did you get those tools from?" I pass the piece over. "Who walks around with a magnifying glass?"

"You never question that in movies, when the hero suddenly pulls out a gun while she was wearing latex all the time," the Pillar says. "Why me?"

"Because we're not in a movie."

The Pillar raises an eyebrow. "Alice, we're characters from a book."

"What?" I am shocked. "Are you saying we're not real?"

"I'm not saying that. I am just pointing out that we've been mentioned in a book that mostly we can't escape. It's like the blueprint of fate of our lives. But never mind, let's focus on the chess piece."

"Anything showing on it?"

"Nothing in particular, but wait…" He pulls the glass magnifier back. "I think it twists open at the middle."

"Really?"

I watch the Pillar give it a couple of tries, then it works. The white queen is split into two pieces, and he pulls out a scrap of paper from inside. "Like a fortune cookie, baby." He looks amused.

"What does it say?"

"It's a note…" He shrugs.

I know why: because it's made of the same yellow note he wrote his Wonder upon—it reminds me that I left my Tiger Lily in a safe box in Marostica and should pick it up soon.

"How come it's the same paper you used for the note you gave me, your Wonder?" I ask the Pillar.

"I don't know. Could be coincidence."

"I don't think so," I say, and then tell him about the Red who saved me earlier today, using the same kind of notes.

"Why not read what's on the note instead of investigating who manufactured it?" the Pillar offers. "It has writing on both sides, actually."

"What does the front say?"

"White Stones."

"Does that mean anything to you?"

"Neither does Black Stones."

"How about the back of the note?"

"Deep Blue."

"This looks like it's going to be a complicated puzzle."

"Deep Blue isn't, actually," the Pillar says. "Assuming all puzzles are chess related, I think I know what it is."

"The suspense is killing me," I mock him. "What is it?"

"Deep Blue is the name of the first IBM computer ever designed to play chess."

"You totally lost me. IBM?" I am not sure how this fits into a puzzle.

"In the nineties, IBM started work on a chess computer, later claiming it could beat a man," the Pillar says. "It was a big scene. Actually, the story I am going to tell you changed mankind's perception of machines."

"I hope it will lead to solving some kind of puzzle."

"In the nineties, IBM challenged the best chess player in the world, at the time, of course, to beat the machine, and he accepted."

"Interesting."

"His name was Garry Kasparov, another Russian chess player—not the Chessmaster, of course."

"And?"

"It's a long story, but let me put it this way: Kasparov eventually lost to the machine after six games and two weeks of an exhausting emotional breakdown."

"Breakdown?"

"IBM played all kinds of psychological tricks on the man to get him to fear the machine."

"Why would they do that?"

"Why do you think, Alice?" The Pillar has one of those smiles on his face again—the one he has when he is about to tell me one of the world's biggest secrets. It reminds me of the time when he told me about food companies making the world fat when we were chasing the Muffin Man.

"Let me guess," I say. "IBM sought propaganda, making their name bigger and getting extreme exposure."

"That's part of it. It was a crucial moment in history, like I said. IBM managed to insinuate into the global conscious brain that the 'machine' *will* beat 'man.'"

"You don't really believe machines will beat us someday?"

"If we create the machine, then it's us who can make it malfunction, Alice. Don't let anyone make you underestimate the fabulousness of being human."

"Enough with the clichés, okay? So why did IBM force Kasparov to lose, really?"

"Before the game, IBM wasn't as big as they are now. They were merely suppliers for Microsoft and such." The Pillar knocks his cane on the ground. "The most important part was: this was just a marketing scheme."

"Marketing for what?"

"For selling millions of chess games," the Pillar says. "Now, everyone wanted to play the IBM model after the game. They wanted to buy it and challenge the game that beat the best chess player in the world."

"Oh. All about money again."

"All about Black Chess, you mean."

"What's Black Chess got to do with this?"

"Black Chess owns IBM, among many other companies all around the world."

"You realize you sound like those lame conspiracy theorists out there?" I tell him. Though I can see Black Chess interfering with everything in the world, some part of me wants to believe the world isn't that manipulated.

"You know what the problem with conspiracy theories is?" the Pillar says.

"Enlighten me." I fold my arms before me.

"They're rarely theories."

I swallow hard, realizing I was only wishfully thinking the world wasn't mostly manipulated by Black Chess. Was that the Bad Alice in me talking again?

"IBM will sue you for such blunt accusations," I tell him.

"They might." Pillar shakes his shoulders. "But they will never win."

"And why is that?"

"Because I am like you, Alice, officially declared mad. I could just apply for a certificate of madness like you. And that's the beauty of it. I'm invincible."

I laugh. "You're right. What's the worst they can do? Send you back to the asylum?"

"Shock therapy until my hair spikes up like an Irish rooster?" He winks.

"I've never realized how blessed we are, being mad." I high-five him.

"Besides, I'm supposed to be a character in a book. They can't sue me. Pillar? Who's the Pillar? The caterpillar from *Alice in Wonderland*? He is real? Get outta here! Now enough play, and back to saving the world," the Pillar says. "We'll start with the Deep Blue clue."

"How so?"

"We'll pay the infamous machine a visit." The Pillar mounts his horse again. "I know where they keep it, and I have a feeling we can beat the machine this time."

Chapter 26

Inspector Dormouse had been sleeping on the couch in the Duchess's office for some time. It hadn't been his plan to fall asleep again. He'd come to discuss an important matter about Professor Pillar. But he couldn't resist the comfort of Margaret Kent's couch in the lobby.

In his sleep he was wondering where he could get a smoother couch for home—or better, for his office at the Department of Insanity. Why weren't such couches available on the market? Even if they were, how could he afford one?

But seriously, the cushions on that couch were so smooth, like marshmallows, like a steady tide of a calm river, swooping left and right. Now that was what he called sleeping. Real sleep, not flashy naps interrupted by his wife or children calling for him so he could wake up and buy the groceries.

What was a man's life without proper sleep? Really? In Inspector Dormouse's head, he sometimes envied sleeping dogs, snoring like they had a stack of a million bones for the rest of their lives. What a feeling!

"You!" A voice woke him up from the sweetest of dreams.

Inspector Dormouse rubbed his eyes, the image of Carolus Ludovicus slowly zooming in. He was so upset to be awake that he grabbed the edges of the couch, in case he had time to sleep again.

"Margaret Kent can't see you," Carolus said. "In fact, no one will. We're all concerned about that Chessmaster in Russia."

"Ah, I see." The inspector stood up and adjusted his clothes. "But I think the identity of Carter Pillar is as important."

"Why? What did you discover?"

"It has to do with the twelve people he killed. They weren't random."

"You already told me on the phone. Elaborate."

"I prefer to talk to Margaret Kent," Inspector Dormouse said.

"Then you'll have to wait, inspector. A long time, so excuse me, because I am supposed to find a way to save our prime minister."

"Mr. Paperwhite?"

"Yes, him. The one the Queen recommended for the position," he said, and walked away.

"Wait," the inspector said. "May I ask why he is called Mr. Paperwhite?" He had considered it weird the prime minister had such a name, especially when it was the name of a character in *Alice Through the Looking Glass*, a man who only wore white papers for clothes.

"Really? You don't get why the Queen calls the prime minister Mr. Paperwhite?"

"Trust me. I gave it a thought, but didn't get it."

"Because he is like a piece of white sheet paper to her—she can write anything she wants on his clothes, and then he'll babble it out on TV, as if they were his own thoughts."

The inspector realized he was grinning, watching Carolus walk away. It was devious, what the Queen did, but the cleverness of it amused him.

He sat back on the couch, preparing himself for another nap. After all, he couldn't leave without telling them who the Pillar really was. It would turn everything that had been happening in the world for the last weeks on its head.

Chapter 27

The Pillar's private plane

It only takes us a couple of hours to get to the Pillar's plane, which he previously parked in a private hangar nearby. It wasn't the mousy chauffeur who was helping this time—the Pillar said he'd let him go home to his family—but another nerdy young man who believed in the evilness of Black Chess.

"Get on the plane," the Pillar tells me. "Before they catch us."

I climb up the stairs, watching the young man throwing me one of those sympathetic looks again. "I pray for you," he says, and I roll my tired eyes one more time.

I am about to scream and pull at my hair when he hands me Tiger Lily's pot, telling me they picked it up from the safe box.

Up on the plane, I strap in next to the Pillar, who is flying this time. He puts on his oversized goggles and wears a helmet with England's flag on it, as if he's riding a motorcycle, not a plane. "I am doing this for my country. You know that, Alice, right?" He sounds like a child with a toy plane, ready to play James Bond.

"All in her majesty's service," I say, playing along.

"You mean the real majesty, right?" He adjusts some levers. "Not the Queen of Hearts. I wonder what happened to real Queen of England."

The plane speeds up on the runway, and we're ready to go wherever the Deep Blue machine is.

"Hang on, Alice," the Pillar says.

"I am." I find my back glued to the seat. "You know how to fly this one, right?"

"I do, but a simple side fact: most plane crashes happen while they take off, so technically getting closer to heaven is the scariest part of the flight."

I close my eyes, and wish I could shut my ears, so I'd stop hearing him yell like a lunatic. As my heart sinks into my feet, the plane wriggles midair for a moment, then my whole inner compass is messed up. I am so confused at what's going on that I am forced to open my eyes again, only to realize the plane is upside down and I am dangling from my seatbelt.

"Had to do it, Alice," the Pillar's upside-down face tells me. His mouth looks really weird that way. "Been dreaming of doing this since…"

"You were a child?"

"No, just a couple of minutes ago."

Finally, he flies the plane back in its normal position.

A few minutes later, I am ready for more questions. "So where do IBM keep the Deep Blue machine now? Where are we going?"

"Let's keep it a surprise," he says. "But know this: Deep Blue hasn't been used since that championship game. Never again. Rumors had it they kept the genius machine in one of the IBM buildings, but later it reappeared in the Computer History Museum in Mountain View, California. They claimed it was a similar one, but it was the real one. For some reason they didn't want to get rid of it, and neither did they want it shown to the public."

"So where is it now?"

"In the last place you could ever think of. You'll see."

I let out a sigh, but I am used to the Pillar's vagueness. What's confusing me is… "What are we actually doing, Pillar?"

"Following the clue."

"To get us where?"

"So we can find Carroll's Knight."

"Which is presumably another chess piece in the shape of a knight?"

"Exactly, part of Lewis Carroll's special chess set, the one Fabiola only knew about."

"And you think the clue in the white queen chess piece will lead us to it?"

"I hope so, or the Chessmaster will kill more world leaders. Who knows what he has in store for us if we don't find it. And don't ask me why he wants it. I have no idea."

"Are you sure we shouldn't try calling Fabiola?"

"She won't talk. I know her."

"You mean you love her." I am being blunt now. "I've read the note you sent to her while she was still in the Vatican."

The Pillar's face dims. No more happy, playful attitude. Even the plane winces a little in his hands. "How did the letter end up in your hands?"

"The March Hare," I say. "He took it on her behalf, because when you sent it, she'd just left the Vatican. Her assistant collected the letter and sent it to the Inklings, where the March read it."

"And the key?"

"It's safe with the March Hare, and Fabiola doesn't know about it. Don't avoid my question. How is it you're in love with Fabiola?"

"I don't want to talk about it." His voice is shattered and weak. He stares ahead, avoids my eyes, and I feel guilty bringing it up.

In that same instant, I receive a message from the March Hare. It's saddening news. The kind of news I shouldn't be telling the Pillar, not now.

"Who's the message from?" the Pillar asks. "Your Red admirer?"

"It's from the March Hare. Something happened to Fabiola."

The Pillar grips the stick harder, still not facing me. He doesn't even ask what happened to her, pretending to be that tough guy who never breaks down.

"She is dying, Pillar," I say as slowly and softly as I can. "Someone poisoned her."

The Pillar says nothing, his knuckles whitening around the flying stick.

"Do you wish to turn back? Maybe you want to see her before she dies."

"No," the Pillar says in a flat voice. "Saving the world from the Chessmaster is more important."

I say nothing. Silence chokes both of us in the cockpit.

"In fact, I feel like doing this again," the Pillar says, and flies the plane upside down again, like a child in pain with too many toys.

Chapter 28

Buckingham Palace, London

The Queen of Hearts had been following the event on TV, as well as awaiting updates from Margaret. The news host announced the latest unfolding events, telling about Alice and the Pillar not finding Carroll's Knight, but a chess piece of a white queen instead. One of the Chessmaster's men had seen them opening the coffin in Marostica, and reported it to the news.

"A white queen chess piece?" the Red Queen said to her dogs, hands on her waist. She didn't care for her guards or advisors at the moment. Whatever was going on seemed beyond anyone's grasp.

She paced her chamber, thinking about the chess piece. If the Chessmaster wanted Carroll's Knight, whatever that was, why did they come across this white queen piece? Was it supposed to really lead Alice and the Pillar to Carroll's Knight? And why would the Chessmaster sacrifice the world to get it?

Her telephone rang. It was Margaret.

"Queen of England speaking," she said, liking the sound of it. In her mind, being the Queen of England seemed cooler than the Queen of Wonderland.

"I know it's you." Margaret sighed. "I called you on your private phone, so it has to be you."

"Oh." The Queen scratched her head. "So tell me, have you found anything out about the Chessmaster?"

"Nothing," Margaret said. "None of us remember him from

Wonderland."

"He said he wasn't a Wonderland Monster."

"Which puzzles me. If he isn't, why lure the Pillar and Alice to find Carroll's Knight? And why do his puzzles scream 'Wonderland'?"

"I agree. He knows a lot about us. Do you think he knows about our plans?"

"I can't say."

"So you're useless like always, Margaret," she said, and kicked her son's head toward her dogs. Her doctors hadn't found a proper way to knit his head to his body again, let alone bring him back to life.

"I'm not," Margaret said. "Something happened to Fabiola a few minutes ago."

"Fabiola?" The Queen of Hearts felt a lump grow bitter in her throat. "What happened?"

"I am sorry to say this, but I think she is dying. It seems she's been poisoned."

"When did this happen?"

"I was waiting for you to ask me this."

"Why?"

Margaret took her time and spoke clearly. "Because our White Queen was poisoned right after Alice and the Pillar found the chess piece, which is that of a…"

"A white queen, too…" The Queen of Hearts slumped in her chair. "Is that supposed to mean something?"

"I can't tell, but it's far from being a coincidence."

Chapter 29

The Pillar's Plane

I am not sure how much I've slept, but when I wake up it seems like more than seven hours have passed. I rub my eyes to take a better look outside my window.

I can't believe what I am seeing.

We're flying low, gliding over a white, snowy mountain in the middle of nowhere. The Pillar next to me is still flying the plane and listening to some Asian chanting melodies.

"Where are we?"

"Beautiful, isn't it?" he says, and keeps chanting *meeha tu tu chi,* or something like that.

"I asked you where we are."

"First, you have to admit it's beautiful."

"Okay, it's beautiful. Where are we?"

"Here." He points at something that's revealing itself in the snow.

I squint and lean forward, waiting for the structures emerging out of the snow to make sense to me. Either my mind refuses to believe it or I am hallucinating.

"Is that a Buddha statue?" I point with an open mouth.

The Pillar nods, pointing. "That one is Buddha, that is Duddha, and the one on the left is Nuddha."

"I've never learned of the last two."

"They're Buddha's sisters, but no one ever mentions them because they were girls. You know how condescending religions are toward women."

I ignore his remark. It's the Pillar. No changing the way he views the world. I keep watching the structure behind the huge statues revealing itself. "It's a monastery?"

"Jackpot!" The Pillar skews the plane, ready to land. "We're in Tibet, baby! I hope you brought your orange robe along."

"You're kidding me."

"We're somewhere near Burang in the Tibet Autonomous Region."

"Why?"

"Why what?"

"Why are we here?"

"This is where IBM keeps their Deep Blue machine," the Pillar says with a happy face, already waving to a few monks waiting for us below.

"Why in here? This seems like the last place on earth to hide such a machine."

"You said it yourself. Bury a genius machine in a monastery in the snow. Genius." He reaches for something in the back with one hand. "Here. You have to get dressed in this."

I grab the monk's cloth. "Do you want me to dress up in this?"

"We have to act like monks or they won't let us see the machine. Trust me, you'll love it here."

Before I have a chance to argue, the plane lands with consecutive thuds on the snow. It's such a clumsy landing that most of our plane's nose is buried in white, and there is something burning in the back.

"My best landing yet," the Pillar says. "The last one, everyone died but me."

Chapter 30

Outside Burang, Tibet Autonomous Region

The beautiful monks welcome us in their orange and red robes as if they haven't seen people outside their tribe in years.

I trot in my new boots the Pillar gave me and feel the chill of cold, though I'm wearing a lot of layers of orange. A few steps closer, I realize the Pillar is still inside the plane.

"Pillar? What's keeping you behind?" I say, turning.

It's only seconds before he appears from behind the plane. He is wearing a lush orange robe and looks pretty much like a Tibetan monk now. Not just because of the robe, but because he's shaved his head bald.

"Seriously?" I grit my teeth.

"I am an expert in communication and we need to blend in. Most monks here are bald, so I figured I should be too."

"Do you know how long it'll take for your hair to grow back?"

"They've got pills for that now," he says. "I didn't like to comb and wash my hair each day anyways. Always wanted to feel the drizzle of water on my bald head in the shower. It was on my bucket list."

A closer look, I realize it's a wig. A bald wig.

Behind us, Tibetans approach us. They speak in a language I don't understand, but an old man, presumably their leader, smiles broadly and holds me gently by the shoulder.

I bow my head with respect, not knowing what to say.

"Alice of Wonderland!" the old man says in English.

"You know me?"

"Who doesn't?" He pulls out a copy of *Through the Looking Glass*, this one with a red cover.

"You've been reading about me?" I am flattered.

"In Chinese!" He shows me that the copy is in their own language. Everything is read from top to bottom instead of left to right. "The monks are crazy about you here."

"Oh." I am speechless, wondering if the monks dismiss their prayers to read a children's book.

The old man nears me, whispering, "The monks spend their time chasing rabbits in the snow, wishing they'd fall into a hole. It's either prayers or rabbit holes around here. I'm Xian, like Xiangqi, named after the Chinese chess game."

"Nice to meet you, Xian," I say. "You have your own chess here?"

"The oldest in the world," he says proudly. "They will tell you the one in Marostica is the oldest, but they don't know squat."

"Squat?" I raise an eyebrow.

"I learned English in Brooklyn, New York." He laughs. "You know our chess game is said to contain the secret of the universe. The Nazis sent their expeditions to Tibet, wanting to find out about it."

"Nazis." I frown. "And squat."

"Or crap." He mirrors my eyebrows.

"So I assume you know this man." I switch my glance toward the Pillar, assuming he may recognize him as the Caterpillar from the books.

The old man turns and faces the bald Pillar, and his smile broadens. "Of course I know him," he says. "Who doesn't know the famous Cao Pao Wong?"

Chapter 31

"Cao Pao Wong?" I glare at the Pillar.

"Better than Kung Fu Panda," the Pillar remarks.

"You were here before?"

"It's a long story." The Pillar changes the subject and turns to Xian. "We need a favor."

"Shoot," Xian says, and I can't fathom his dialect or slang. Maybe he is some sort of a modern monk.

"We have a puzzle that led us to you." The Pillar shows him the note we found in the chess piece.

"Sticky note!" Xian seems fascinated with it. He sticks it on his head. "Haven't seen one of those in about...hmmm...forty years."

"I'll send you a tank full of sticky notes later," the Pillar says. "As you can see, it has the words *Deep Blue* written on one side."

"*White Stones* on the other," Xian says.

"Let's stick to the part you know about," the Pillar says.

"You mean the machine?" Xian looks all serious and worried.

The Pillar nods.

"You remember what the machine looks like, right?"

"Of course," the Pillar says. "A long, monolith-like black box. Inside it are all the wires and microchips that make it think."

"Good memory, Cao Pao Wong."

"I think the puzzle is a secret way to open it."

"No one has been able to open the machine ever before. I hope you remember that."

"I know; even the guys at IBM believed it was haunted when they couldn't open it after the game with Kasparov. Just tell me where you keep it."

Xian rubs his chin. "This is going to be a bit of a problem."

"Why so?" I interrupt.

"Like the Pillar said, it looks like a monolith—black, intimidating, and huge. You look at it and feel strange and conflicting emotions."

"So?" I ask.

"Let me put it this way," Xian says. "It looks like the monolith in that *Space Odyssey* movie by Stanley Kubrick."

I haven't seen the movie, so the Pillar explains it's about space exploration, where a mysterious monolith is found by astronauts. The monolith is shown in the movie to have taught the first man, apes precisely, how to hunt and make a weapon. In brief, it showed man how to make things, from a hunting weapon to a thinking computer in our modern day.

"I get it," I tell Xian. "So the IBM machine looks like that monolith in the movie. What does this have to do with us seeing Deep Blue now?"

Xian takes a moment and then says, "Well, my monks are now worshiping the machine in the middle of the snow."

Chapter 32

Xian walks us to where the Deep Blue machine sticks out of the snow. It's about two meters high and slightly less than a meter wide. It also looks like it parts from the middle, only if you punch in a combination of secret numbers in the digital pad on top. A sixteen-number combination.

"So the issue is to how to get the numbers?" the Pillar asks Xian.

"I'd call it your secondary issue," Xian says. "The first would be them." He points at the monks in orange praying while facing the monolith. A few of them are already suspicious about us.

"So they think Deep Blue is God?" I ask.

"Todd," Xian says.

"Todd?" the Pillar asks.

"Yes, Todd," Xian says.

"Who's Todd?" I ask Xian.

"God," Xian says.

"Todd is God?" the Pillar asks.

"Or God is Todd," I remark, loving the insanity.

"How can God be Todd?" the Pillar asks.

"A misspelling," Xian says.

"You Buddhists misspelled God's name?" the Pillar says.

"Not at all," Xian says. "One day, I took my monks to New York. They asked a man whom New Yorkers pray to. A drunk man on a Sunday morning told them 'God' in a slurry tongue. They thought he said Todd. And since Deep Blue is a computer, and my monks believe computers are western inventions, they called it Todd."

"What about Deep Blue?" I ask.

"You can't worship something called Deep Blue," Xian says.

"Why even worship a machine?" I ask. "Are you sure you guys are Buddhists?"

"First of all, not all of my monks worship Todd. Some of them don't. Secondly, we're not really Buddhists; we're left out in the cold wearing those silly orange robes, and we don't know why we do it. We were just born that way."

"And third?"

"That part of my men worship Todd so they can get an American visa."

"What?" My voice pitches up.

"They were told that if they worshiped a machine from California, and the machine liked them, they'd end up with an American visa."

"That's nonsense."

"A green card, maybe?" Xian scratches his head.

"You're being outrageously offensive right now," I tell him, about to tell those poor monks the truth.

"Work permit?" Xian asks. "They wouldn't mind that. It's really cold and lonely here."

"Stop it." I hold my head to stop it from internally exploding. "Who the hell told these poor monks they could get a visa by worshiping a machine?"

Xian shrugs, looking sideways.

"Who?" I get his attention by grabbing his robe.

"Him." He points at the Pillar.

I turn and find the Pillar is already praying with the monks, avoiding me. When I near him, he is talking a woman into marrying him and giving her British citizenship, which is way cooler than American.

Chapter 33

It's hard to do something about the Pillar's atrocious behavior right now. I don't even know when he was here in the past or what he's done. All I get from his wink is that he is distracting the monks so I can solve the machine's puzzle.

"Come with me, Xian," I tell the old man, walking back to Deep Blue.

"So you know how the numbers go to the machine?" he asks.

"Hardly," I say, looking at the note again. "All I know is that the other side of the note should be the way to do it."

"White stones?" Xian asks.

"Do you have any idea what it means?"

"I am trying to think."

"If Lewis—or Fabiola, or whoever designed this global puzzle— meant the 'white stones' to help us open the machine, then it should point at something nearby."

"We're in the middle of nowhere. There is nothing nearby."

He is right. My eyes dart back to the machine itself. I notice the back of the machine is divided into small squares, carved with a sharp tool. Many, but not all, of the squares have circles inside them.

"What is this, Xian?"

"We've never known exactly. It came with the machine."

"Looks like a calendar to me. The squares." I rub my hands on its surface. "Look at the top of each set—you can see those small writings. Monday, Tuesday, Wednesday, and so on."

"One of our monks suggested that, but what use could it be?"

"I agree. It seems useless, but why write a calendar on the back of the machine?"

"You tell me, Alice of Wonderland. Maybe you can autograph my robe?"

"Autograph?" I roll my eyes. "What would you tell others? That the girl from the book autographed it? Stick with the puzzle, please."

"As you say, Alice of Wonderland," he says, and pulls out a pair of slippers from under his robe. They're made to look like two rabbits. "Can't think of a better occasion for wearing them. Brought them from—"

"New York, I know. You should stop being obsessed with American products."

"But the slippers aren't American," he argued. "They're made in Wonderland, the beautiful salesman told me."

I roll my eyes again, wondering just how many more foolish and stupid people I'll be running into. Then I grab one of the slippers and check the label on the back. "It's made in China, Xian," I say. "So you technically let some sneaky salesman sell you an American product, claiming it was from Wonderland, when probably one of these monks manufactured it."

Xian looks shocked. "You mean I could've already obtained the American visa with those rabbit slippers?"

I leave him be and take another look at the calendar. Some of the squares are marked. Some with a white circle. Some with black. The scene reminds me of the War between the Inklings and Black Chess, and the black and white chessboard of life.

"I found you a white stone." Xian shows up again. He hands me a snowball. "You said it had to do with something nearby. A snowball looks like a stone and is white."

Though I dismiss his suggestion, I realize it gave me a clue. The white circles in the calendar could be the white stones. But how are they related to discovering the numbers that open the machine?

"Pillar?" I shout against the sudden wind looming nearby.

He doesn't answer me, still having fun with the monks and promising them visas and better lives.

"Cao Pao Wong?"

"Yes, dear," he says with a nose smudged in snow.

"What do white stones and calendars have in common?"

And there he suddenly looks interested. "Why did you mention calendars now?"

"There is a calendar drawn on the back with white circles."

"So this is it." He clicks his fingers and approaches.

"Is what?"

"The clue." He stands next to me and Xian. "Nice slippers, Xian," he comments. "I know a guy in the States who has the originals from Wonderland."

Xian looks double shocked.

"What do you mean this is the clue?" I ask the Pillar.

"Lewis Carroll had a fascination with marking days on calendars," the Pillar says. "And he always marked the happy day in his life with white stones."

"Is that true?"

"I never lie on Tuesdays,"

"Wednesday," I say.

"Then I never lie on Wednesdays." He winks and stares at the calendar. "Now tell me you figured out the numbers already."

"I can't seem to get the connection." But then I regret speaking so fast, because one more glance helps me figure it out. Each white stone marks a particular number in each month. Starting from the third day, ninth, eleventh, and so on. There are sixteen numbers in all.

"Genius puzzle," the Pillar says.

I punch the digits in while the Pillar distracts the monks, and hurray, the door clicks open. Xian helps me pull it back. It's a bit heavy, and inside there is nothing but wires and...

Wait. There it is. Another chess piece.

Chapter 34

World Chess Championship, Moscow, Russia

"Where are Alice and the Pillar?" the Chessmaster asked, just after making four consecutive moves with four different presidents. He seemed to have a certain love for white knights in the game. He used them a lot, leaving world leaders in total awe of his brilliant moves.

"Untraceable so far," one of his men told him.

"How is that possible? If they've found the white queen chess piece, they must have been told of the next clue. And if so, I assume they will need transportation. The pieces are scattered all over the world."

The Chessmaster's assistant said nothing, afraid to upset him.

"Why do you need this Carroll's Knight so much?" uttered one of the world leaders. His name was Samson, declared dictator and sultan of Madderstan, a neighboring country to Looneystan.

"What did you just ask me?" The Chessmaster rose and rubbed the right side of his mustache.

"You heard me." Samson seemed full of himself, unlike most world leaders.

"You think you can just ask me questions because your country is a terrorism-spreading little land?" The Chessmaster knew Samson pretty well. The dictator ruled a small, but oil-rich, country in Africa, and his small tribe of soldiers endorsed terrorism everywhere, just for the fun of it.

"Guilty as charged." Samson raised his hands in the air. "I am such a bully. I love hurting other people and enforcing my ideologies on them by the sound of the gun. But how different are you?"

The Chessmaster rubbed the left side of his mustache and approached Samson. He could see the man had already made six moves, one move away from a checkmate, one move away from drinking the seventh cup and getting poisoned.

"You think I am just a lowlife like you?" the Chessmaster said.

Samson laughed. "What else are you? Just another madman, thinking the world is not enough of a price for his ego."

The Chessmaster reached for the knight on the chessboard and made the move. It was an easy one in his book, though not expected by any of his spectators.

Samson didn't bother. He reached for his poisoned drink. "My men will slice you to pieces after I die, Chessmaster."

Before he gulped, the Chessmaster gripped his wrist. "You have no idea who I am. You have no idea why I am doing this. All you are is a cockroach of a human being; a parasite, spreading chaos in the world and making it a terrible place."

"And again, how different can you be?" Samson asked.

"I am the world's salvation," the Chessmaster said, and forced the drink down the dictator's throat.

The dictator dropped next to his table in an instant. The world broadcast the scene, showing him wriggling and writhing before his death.

The Chessmaster turned and faced the camera. "I just killed another world leader. Don't think I won't go killing more. And let me tell you this: every one of you is responsible for finding Alice and the Pillar now. Find them and bring them back to me, or your world leaders will not be saved."

The words echoed the right way in the Chessmaster's head. He demonstrated people's worst fears and knew they would cooperate immediately. His message should have had the desired effect, but then his assistant pointed at the news on TV talking about what just happened.

To the Chessmaster's surprise, people were leaving their houses searching for Alice and the Pillar. But not because they feared him. On the contrary—they had just declared their respect for the Chessmaster killing one of the world's cruelest dictators.

It all left the Chessmaster bewildered. He sensed that warmth in his heart, the kind of warmth that had left him years ago. People suddenly believed he was their savior. He'd killed the world leader that most of them wanted dead already. Not all of them, of course, but enough people to help him catch Alice and the Pillar.

But the Chessmaster, being the dark being he was, also wasn't fond of people's love. He didn't like to feel empathy or being admired. He'd transcended such weak emotions long ago. He needed to breathe anger and talk in vengeful syllables, or he'd weaken before completing his mission. The one he'd been planning since the fourteenth of January, 1898.

Chapter 35

Tibet

"It's a rook." I grip it and show it to the Pillar.

"Second piece of the puzzle," the Pillar says. "I bet you can unscrew it open."

"I can." I am still looking at the mysterious piece. "Is this also made of Lewis's bones?"

"Without a doubt."

"You think it will lead us to Carroll's Knight?"

"Eventually."

"What do you mean?"

"Remember when I told you I think I know what's going on with the Chessmaster, back in the tomb in Marostica?" the Pillar says.

But before we have a chance to discuss his theory, I realize the monks are surrounding us from all directions.

"What's going on, Xian?" I ask the old man.

"I believe Cao Pao Wong knows." Xian hides behind the Deep Blue machine.

The monks look angry now, balling fists against fists, making creepy faces, and murmuring angry words I can't understand.

"Pillar?" I say worriedly.

"Do you still know None Fu, Alice?" the Pillar asks, taking a strange martial arts position, reminding me of Kermit the Frog.

"Why are you asking?" I say.

The answer materializes in the monks readying themselves in warrior positions. All at once. They're mastering the hardest position I once saw in Jack's None Fu book.

"I hope you can deal with orange belts in None Fu." The Pillar shrugs, taking a None Fu position himself now.

"I have reached the highest levels in the future, but right now I think I still am a blue belt."

"Blue belt isn't good enough," the Pillar says. "Orange belts will kick your sorry little butt in the air, somersault you, and lay you down on a sword."

"So what are we going to do? Why do the monks want to kill us? Don't tell me it's because of the visa."

"Part of it," the Pillar says. "They must've realized I played them."

"Which makes it time to tell me what you were doing here before."

"I know why he was here before." Xian raises a hand from behind the machine.

"Speak up, Xian," I demand.

"Cao Pao Wong is—I mean was our…"

"Your what?"

"None Fu master," Xian exclaims. "He taught the village the art of None Fu years ago, so we could face our enemies."

"You know None Fu?" I glare at the Pillar.

"Used to. Frankly, I can't None Fu anything at the moment."

"You forgot None Fu?" Xian is shocked for the hundredth time. "That's impossible."

"Stick with me, Xian." I steady myself and breathe, eyes on the slowly approaching monks. "Why would they want to kill us if Cao Pao Wong was their None Fu master?" I am not accepting answers from the

Pillar at the moment.

"Because it turned out not to be None Fu," Xian says.

"Don't confuse the *fu* out of me, Xian. I am not following."

"I needed money, and I was lost in snow, being hunted down by an old enemy of mine," the Pillar says. "I needed the monks to trust me and help me travel out of this frozen land, so I played them and taught them None Fu."

"Which wasn't really None Fu," Xian elaborates, scratching his head. "When the monks used his technique against the wolves threatening our families each winter, they all died. That's why the Pillar shaved his head; so they wouldn't recognize him. He had hair then."

"That's why." I sigh. "Why am I not surprised?" I tell the Pillar.

One of the monks approaches me and speaks in English. "None of this is why we're going to kill you."

"Your accent is great." The Pillar flashes a thumbs-up. "Pretty sure you'll get the visa."

"Shut up," the orange monk says. "We know you fooled us, but we're civilized and forgiving people."

"That's definitely a bonus for getting the visa with today's hostility and terrorism." The Pillar doesn't stop. "America's big on forgiveness—and mac and cheese, of course."

"I told you to shut up," the monk roars. "We'll kill you because we've been waiting for someone to solve and open the machine and find the chess piece for years."

"Now that's truly civilized," I scoff.

"She is badass, by the way." The Pillar points at me. "You really don't want to mess with her. She's escaped an asylum. Killed her friends, her boyfriend, and a man who did nothing but sell muffins. She is brutal. A killing machine. No conscience at all. I dare you: if you can, kill her first."

"Pillar!" I clench my fists.

"No need for games," the monk says. "Hand us the chess piece or die."

"You mean we won't die if we hand it over?" I ask.

"No, you will die either way." The monk shakes his head. "I just see them say it like that in the movies."

Suddenly, the Pillar panics and stares at something in the sky behind the monks. "Look!" He points with all the fear of the world in his eyes. "A flying Buddha!"

"Really?" The monks turn for a second, and the Pillar kicks one of them unconscious, then another.

The monks are still looking upward, and I wonder what's so interesting about a flying Buddha, if there was ever one.

The Pillar flattens the two unconscious men on their stomach, and pushes them near a steep, snowy slope, then sits upon one. "Sit on yours," he says. "Time to ski. Kinda."

I do, but the other monks have already figured out the Pillar's silly Buddha trick. They start trotting after us in the snow.

The Pillar and I are already gliding down the slope of snow, too fast.

"We'll get you, Cao Pao Wong!" the monks scream behind us.

"Villains always say that at the end of movies," the Pillar shouts back. "It never works, even if there's a sequel."

Chapter 36

Margaret Kent's office, Westminster Palace

"I want to know the connection between Fabiola's poisoning and the white queen chess piece, right now." Margaret rapped on her desk.

Carolus shrugged, but the Cheshire didn't. He had possessed a rabbit now. Enough with the politicians and humans, he'd thought. A talking rabbit amused him much more.

"We're on it, Duchess," Carolus said. "But it's really hard to find a plausible connection."

"I don't take no for answer," Margaret said. "This is too mysterious. I need to know what the Chessmaster is up to."

"I say he is up to end the world as we know it," the Cheshire said. His voice was squeaky and he sniffed between words. His rabbit nose was running as if he had a flu, and his eyes were funny. He stared at everything in such excitement, as if it were a miracle, especially the carrot in front of him.

"I didn't permit you to speak, Cheshire," Margaret roared.

"As you wish, Duchess. Carrots?" he offered. "Good for the temper—and ugly women."

"I thought they were good for the eyes," Carolus said.

"I can't speak because the Duchess told me not to," the Cheshire said.

"But you *are* speaking," Carolus argued.

"I could stop speaking if you stop asking." The Cheshire grinned with the rabbit's mouth, which was creepy.

"Stop it!" Margaret said, reading a message she'd just received on her mobile phone. "I'm told the Pillar and Alice are in China. They found a second piece, part of the puzzle."

"China!" the Cheshire said. "Never had Chinese carrots."

Margaret dismissed him. "The next piece is a rook," she told Carolus.

"A rook?" Carolus asked. "And a white queen. Hmmm, I have no idea what this means."

"Neither do I," Margaret began, but then she suddenly felt ill, and clutched her stomach.

"You pregnant?" The Cheshire chewed on his carrot.

"She looks ill," Carolus said.

Margaret had lost her speech. The pain inside her was too strong and sudden. She reached out, but the Cheshire gripped tighter to the carrot and refused to share. She reached out to Carolus and he stuck his head forward, wondering if this was some kind of dance.

Margaret dropped speechless on the floor with a thud.

"Is she dead?" Carolus said.

"I think she was poisoned." The Cheshire puffed the carrot like a pipe. "In fact, I think what happened to Fabiola just happened to her, too."

"Are you saying Fabiola's poisoning has something to do with them finding the white queen?" The Cheshire shook his rabbit's foot. "And Margaret's poisoning has something to do with them finding the rook?"

Chapter 37

Tibet

As we glide all the way down to the bottom of the snow, all kinds of questions present themselves. What's really going on? Why are we supposed to find Carroll's Knight, and why does the Chessmaster need it? Most of all, who is the Chessmaster?

I end up hitting a bump in the snow and skewing to the right, where I hit into the Pillar. Both of us hang on to each other, balling up like a huge snowball that is rolling deeper into the pit of the hill.

The way down reminds me of my journey with the Pillar. We're both unusual persons with secrets only few people know about—me with what's still locked in my memory, and the Pillar with whatever grand plan he has in store for me and himself.

But in any case, and even when he proves to be a mad person by the minute, I am stuck with him, just like we're stuck now. Not because I can't do it any other way, but because behind the masquerade of being a one-in-a-million nutty professor, I am sure he always has my back.

Speaking of backs, I almost crushed mine when we stopped right now.

"Better than a Disney roller coaster," the Pillar comments, standing up.

The monks at the top of the hill stand in a circle, too scared to follow us down. As much as we've escaped them, I don't see how we're going to get out of here.

"We're trapped down here," I say.

"Pretty much." He looks around. "Too bad gravity doesn't allow people to fall up. Why do we all have to fall down and never up? I never understood."

"Why would anyone want to fall up?" I smack the snow off my clothes.

"Are you kidding me? Fall up to the stars, to the skies. I'd love to fall up in another life."

"Whatever." I put my hands on my waist. "So, since we might never get out of here, at least tell me what your theory is."

"What theory?"

"You said you thought you understood what was going on with the Chessmaster when we were up there."

"Ah, that. Look, it's seems like we're not just on a journey to find Carroll's Knight."

"Then what?"

"We're collecting chess pieces, one by one, and the last will probably be Carroll's Knight."

"Sounds plausible. Are you suggesting we're collecting Carroll's whole set, the one he had Fabiola make from his bones?"

"I assume so. And since Fabiola can't tell us what it was for, we'll have to struggle with finding out why."

"Are you sure Fabiola doesn't know the Chessmaster?"

"No, I am not, but how can I be sure?"

"Are you sure you don't know who the Chessmaster is?"

"Other than the rumor that they say his name is *Vozchik Stolb*, no, nothing."

"It's a Russian name, right?"

"Yes, but I'm not sure what it means."

"So you think we're really going to look for all the chess pieces?"

"Not all, or it will take us forever." The Pillar tries to make out what the monks' shouts mean. "I believe we're collecting the major pieces. Queen, king, rook, bishop, pawn, and knight. One of each."

There is a thud somewhere nearby, and the monks' voices pitch higher.

"What are they saying?" I ask the Pillar.

"Giant," the Pillar says. "The giant is coming."

And that's when a door in the snowy mountain's side slides open and a huge man appears.

Chapter 38

The giant man has thick, hairy skin, like an ape. He is seven or eight feet tall. His eyebrows are as thick as the bushy hair on his chest. He only wears shorts, and the diameter of his leg is the breadth of me and the Pillar combined. His hand is huge.

"Sorry we woke you up," the Pillar says.

"You know him?" I clamp my back against the wall.

"No, and I don't want to."

It's clear to me that the giant has his eyes on the Pillar. Each thud in the snow shakes the place all around us. Snowflakes sprinkle off the earth and into the air.

"So the monks had a plan B," I say.

"Plan death, I'd say." The Pillar apparently has no means to fight with the speechless giant. "I'd start climbing up if I were you, Alice."

"And leave you here?"

"Climb up or die. One of us has to distract him. Go."

It's not like there is an easy way to climb up, but I get the Pillar's concern. I don't even have a chance to use my None Fu with the giant.

Then something out of this world happens.

"Hit me," the Pillar says to giant.

"Are you crazy?" I say.

"Hit me, you big, ugly cannonball!"

The giant accepts the invitation and lashes the back of his arm into the Pillar, who flies through the air and then thuds against the snow wall to the left.

"Stop it, Pillar. Don't encourage him. I'm sure you can trick him with your smooth tongue."

The Pillar doesn't listen to me. "Is that all you've got?" he sneers at the big man.

Another lash, to the right this time. The way the Pillar slides down from the wall after this is almost like a cartoon.

Blood spatters on the snow and the Pillar pulls himself up, stretches his neck, and says, "Try a better one."

I can't believe my eyes as the giant punches the Pillar for the third time. This time he almost buries him an inch deeper into the snow.

The Pillar spits out the blood and grins. "Not so hard, stupid," he tells the giant. "You don't want to kill me. You want to have fun with me."

The silent giant grimaces, not sure why he shouldn't want to kill the Pillar.

"Because let's face it. You're a giant schmuck living alone in this hole in the ground. You're lonely and have no one to talk to. Your IQ is probably lower than the temperature, so why kill me right away when you can have a good time doing it slower?"

The giant grins, liking the idea, and begins a series of small hits at the Pillar.

I try to talk him out of it, but he insists I climb up. And right there, when I don't know how to do it, a rope dangles down for me, and I cling to it.

"Typical of Hollywood movies," I mumble. "To have a *deus ex machina* save you in the last minute."

The Pillar is still being hit, for the seventh time, I believe, and someone is pulling the rope up. I hope it's not the monks, because why would they want to help me?

I feel guiltier as I am being lifted up, leaving the Pillar behind. Am I really going to let him die?

Then a terrible thought suddenly hits me. "Pillar!" I scream while being lifted up. "Who is it who is going to kill you in the future?"

The Pillar cranes his neck for a brief moment. Amidst all the punching he is suffering, his eyes speak the truth to me. I get it now. I understand why he visited the hospice instead of facing his killer. "Don't tell me it's me who's going to kill you."

The Pillar smiles, and slightly nods, as if he doesn't want to tell me but has to. "And now I know how."

Above me, the monks' voices are absent, and the thin beam of sunlight seems like a dagger of light killing me. I decide to let go of the rope and jump down and help the Pillar. "If you think I'd kill you by leaving you to die by the hands of the giant, you're mistaken." I spit snow from my mouth. "The future can be changed. I am never going to kill you."

But right there, when I'm about to jump back down, a firm hand pulls me up. I resist, craning my head up. "Let go of me," I cry.

But then I realize I can't fight this grip, because it's the kind of hand that's too strong for me. It's the Dude's.

Chapter 39

"Leave me alone!" I shout at the Dude in the Red outfit, but his grip is like a steel chain. "I have to save the Pillar."

In his silence, as usual, the Dude passes me another note, and I am already fed up with those: *It's his time. Leave him be.*

"No, I won't," I say, still trying to find my way back down, but a swirl of winding snow has already covered the hole below and I can't see anything.

Another note: *It's the price you will have to pay for saving Jack.*

I turn and glare at him. "How do you know about Jack?"

It doesn't matter. What you need to know is that's part of the laws of time-traveling. If you cheat time and save Jack, time will demand an equal sacrifice.

"What does that mean?"

Time will take the Pillar's life for Jack's, Alice, and there is nothing you can do about it.

"The hell with time!"

You don't know what you're talking about. Time is the one thing that lasts while we all die eventually.

"But why should I be the one to kill the Pillar?"

Because you're the one who saved Jack. Cheat time and enjoy a dear person's resurrection, but pay the price and live with another dear person's loss.

"So time knows how much the Pillar really means to me," I tell myself.

Now take a breath, and give it up. The Pillar is gone. I killed the monks, by the way. We're leaving soon.

It's hard to really accept this, but the wind is stirring quite strongly, and my survival instincts take over. The Pillar's death is shoved to the back of my head, though I can't believe I am really doing this.

Next to me, I see monks spread dead on the ground. "Where did you come from?" I ask.

I'm British, from Kent.

"You know I didn't mean it that way," I say. "Did you follow me? Why are you helping me?"

No note this time, because the Pillar's pain below is tearing me apart.

"Another hit, sweet, big, stupid thing," I hear the Pillar roar at the giant from below—at least he is not dead yet.

I turn to the Dude. "Can I ask you a favor?"

Anything you want.

"Help him." I point to the Pillar below.

No. The Pillar isn't on your side, anyways.

"What do you care? Didn't you say you'd do anything I want?"

Anything you want that's always in your best interest.

"This man cares for me," I insist.

He surely may act so, but you don't really know what his grand plan is.

"Look, others have warned me of him before. They're all wrong."

Again, my words are interrupted by the Pillar's pain.

The Dude points at a hot air balloon he has ready in the distance. It seems like this is his escape plan.

"I am not leaving the Pillar," I say.

You have to stop the Chessmaster.

"Like I don't know that? I need to save the Pillar first."

He is a lunatic, asking the giant to keep hitting him.

"I know." I sigh. "I wonder why he is doing this."

The Dude churns out another note: *Alice, listen to me: you have to stop the Chessmaster. You have no idea who he is.*

This gets my attention. "You know who the Chessmaster is?"

I do. He is the scariest man on earth. Only you can stop him.

"Enough with the puzzles. Who is the Chessmaster?"

The Dude points at the balloon and writes a note: *Get in the balloon and I will tell you all about him.*

I turn and look at poor Pillar, then back at the Dude. I am torn with what the right thing to do is. But I am so curious about the Chessmaster.

The Dude passes me another note. This one is prewritten. It's the size of a letter.

"What is this?" I ask.

The story of who the Chessmaster is.

Chapter 40

The Dude disappears into a storm of snow, as the wind begins to swirl all around me. It's a sudden and extreme change in the weather, as if unseen forces in the universe want to prevent me from reading the note.

I duck on all fours and clamp the note, trying to read it under the safety of my orange hood, still faintly hearing the Pillar's pain. There is hardly anything I can do about it now, but I wish the wind would weaken the giant's punches.

Underneath the protective hood I begin reading the note. There are two separate parts, actually, and even under the hood they are still hard to read it in any detail.

The first note is written in old English. It almost has the tone of fairy tales or formal old English letters.

Skimming through, it talks about an eternal war between black and white. The black calling themselves Black Chess; the white, the Inklings. The note mentions it as a prediction, since at the time of writing—probably a long, long time ago—the two forces had no names.

The two forces are said to originate in Elfland, which a man by Lewis Carroll may change into Wonderland. The forces have no boundaries. They will kill and fight for as long it takes until they find the Six Impossible Keys.

The wind throws me off balance. I tense my knees and then fall on my stomach, waiting for it to leave me alone. Even flattened on the ground I arch my back a little and keep reading using the weak light of my phone.

The note later mentions the Six Impossible Keys are used to unlock something, but not a door, nor is it a box. It unlocks the one thing no man can unlock—whatever that means.

But then it gets weirder—or clearer; I am not sure. The note talks about the Six Impossible Keys being useless without the Looking Glass.

This tells of the Looking Glass again, but fails to mention why it's important—unless it's simply a mirror and I am reading too much into things.

Another howl of wind attacks me. I can still hear the Pillar struggling with the giant in the distance.

I bite the second note, clinging to it with my teeth, as I am about to finish reading the first one.

Only two paragraphs left.

The next sentences talk about a crucial point in the journey to unlock the Six Keys. One milestone is when a third force, neither black nor white, threatens to end the world before the Wonderland Wars begin. That one is called the Chessmaster, who is almost invincible. He is a monster of pain, created by accident, out of an unholy spell used by two irresponsible Wonderlanders.

I shrug, reading this, trying to put two and two together, but nothing comes to mind. It's all too vague to comprehend, still.

Only the last two sentences show me what's in store. The first explains that the Chessmaster needs to find a "missing piece"—I assume it's the chess pieces we're collecting now—to protect himself.

Protect himself? The Chessmaster is doing all this to protect himself? How can that be? Protect himself from what?

The revelation comes as a shock in the last sentence.

The Chessmaster desperately needs the chess piece of a knight, made from Lewis Carroll's bone, so he can play the last chess game in mankind's history. A game that will either protect him from a great evil or initiate the apocalypse.

I am at a loss for words, hardly imagining what kind of chess game the note means. I can accept the idea of a final chess game that will end the world—in a most Wonderlastic nonsensical way, of course. But what does the Chessmaster want to protect himself from?

Between the terrible wind kicking at my arched back and the Pillar's struggles below, I part my teeth and let the second note fall into my hands. This one tells the story of who the Chessmaster really is.

Chapter 41

Buckingham Palace

The Queen listened to Carolus's story about what happened to Margaret, and couldn't fathom what was going on.

"She just fell like Fabiola?" she asked.

"Yes, my Queen," Carolus said.

"But if Fabiola dropped because of the appearance of the white queen chess piece, why would Margaret fall after discovering the rook piece?"

"It's puzzling," Carolus said. "We're not sure our theory is right, but the two women got ill after each piece was discovered."

"That's nonsense," the Queen said. "What is this, witchcraft, where you kill a person by poking needles and pins into a puppet?"

"A chess piece, this time."

"How could they possibly be connected to a chess piece?" the Queen snarled. "I am not buying this. Are you sure Margaret and Fabiola aren't faking it?"

"I suppose they're not. Fabiola is doing pretty badly. A special committee of doctors are on her case, flying her to the best medical centers across Europe."

The Queen paced around her chamber, hands behind her back, trying to put reason to this unreasonable world. "Assuming the chess pieces are so powerful, we need to know who the Chessmaster is."

"We must," Carolus said. "He is beginning to scare me."

The Queen's telephone rang. It was Mr. Jay, so she dismissed Carolus and answered.

"What can I do for you, Mr. Jay?"

"Things are getting complicated," he said.

"I assume your men failed in catching Alice?"

"True, but it turns out that Alice is the least of my worries at the moment."

"How so?"

"My men discovered the true identity of the Chessmaster."

"And?" The Queen shrugged.

"It's not good news."

"Is he a Wonderland Monster?"

"It's hard to tell."

"But you said you know his identity."

"And that's the problem. The Chessmaster did something in the past, in Wonderland, that's too scary to imagine."

"So he did live in Wonderland, among us?"

"Yes and no."

"I'm puzzled, Mr. Jay. Who is the Chessmaster?"

"Let me read his story for you," Mr. Jay said.

"Read his story?"

"It was written by Lewis Carroll's sister, part of his lost diaries."

"Why hasn't Lewis written it himself? I'm so confused."

"You'll get it once I finish reading the story. Let me begin with its title."

"It's a diary entry with a title?"

"Yes. The title is a number: 14011898."

"Is that the date of—"

"Yes, now don't interrupt me, and listen."

Chapter 42

Lewis Carroll's diary. An entry written by his sister in Guildford, United Kingdom, on the fourteenth of January, 1898

As I write this, my lovely brother Lewis is dying in his room in my house at Guildford. He's been here for some time due to his recent illnesses—mostly the intensifying migraines and the possibility of being schizophrenic.

I haven't seen much of his split persona that he claims to encounter. On the contrary, my brother's presence has been so pleasant that I regret not having spent more time with him earlier in life.

He will die a bachelor, but having affected every child in the world with his books—and, of course, he can't stop talking about that girl who inspired him to write the books, Alice.

But I am not here to complain about my brother. I am here to write about what just happened and what I saw with my own eyes. Better write it right away before my fragile old memories escape me.

Let's start with Lewis having been obsessed with chess since he went to Russia many years ago. He couldn't get it out of his head that he had to write *Through the Looking Glass*, the sequel to *Alice in Wonderland*, based around a game of chess.

Ever since he arrived from Oxford to my modest two-storey house here, he's had his own chessboard.

It's been set up and ready on a table next to his bed for some time. Every time I asked him about whom he was expecting to play with, he laughed wearily and told me he was expecting an opponent to arrive any moment.

I never understood; neither did I pay much attention to it. I was ignorant about chess and Lewis had always been an unusual man. You don't ask him about what he is doing, for he is like a child who does what he wants when he wants.

In the last few days, his health had deteriorated much, and it was devastating watching him like that. He sometimes joked that I need not worry because he would not die, not until he played that last chess game with his expected opponent.

Which made it harder for me to hold my tears, because I thought he was hallucinating.

But the expected guest came.

It was late at night when the doors to my balcony sprang open due to a snowy wind with an aggressive appetite for destruction. I stood up, locked the window back, and was about to go back to bed when I heard Lewis talking to someone.

Tiptoeing, I approached his room and could instantly see that Lewis had left the bed and sat at the table for a game of chess. Opposite him sat the awaited, and most unwelcome, guest. I couldn't see his face, though, not from this angle. All I was sure of was that he was wearing a red cloak.

"I thought you would play the game, using your special chess pieces, carved from your own bones," the guest said to my brother Charles—I mean Lewis, as most of you know him by that name.

"I knew you'd ask for them, but you will never find them," Lewis said. "I've had someone help me keep them away from you."

"Nothing is that far away, Carroll," the guest said. "I will find the set. I will find the knight, eventually."

"Then it will take you years and years to do so, because I scattered them all over the world."

"The world is mine, not yours," said the guest. "I have time; you have none."

"Don't get carried away. You haven't beaten me yet."

"No one has ever beaten me when their time came, Lewis."

"There is a first for everything."

"My first will also be my last."

"And it scares you." Lewis looked unusually competitive. I wondered who the guest was.

"It does scare me," answered the guest. "But when it happens, I remind myself that I never lose. It just never happened, because I am—"

"No need to tell me your real name." Lewis raised a hand. "I've known your name since the days of Wonderland."

It was sentences like these that made me doubt my brother's sanity. He had lost his grip on reality, thinking Wonderland was real. But the guest didn't seem to object.

"If only I had enough time in Wonderland," said the guest. "I'd have killed so many."

"But it still wouldn't be enough," Lewis remarked. "Because your sickness of killing is unquenchable. Blood will never taste like wine from Eden, no matter how much you spill."

"You know I have the right to do what I do."

"I sympathised with you in the beginning, but no more."

"Why? Because you know it's her who made me what I am?"

"Leave *her* out of it," Lewis said, and made his first chess move. That was when I noticed the small cups of liquor on both sides of the board. With each move, they had to follow up with one drink.

At some point I was going to enter the room, but then Lewis discreetly waved me off. I respected his wishes and stood watching, still wondering about the guest cloaked in red.

Later it was clear that Lewis was losing. What troubled me was the fear showing on his face with every move. It was unreasonable, not the kind of fear that shows in a game of chess, no matter what the price.

But the cloaked guest had another opinion. Close to Lewis's seventh move, the guest was laughing. "Tell me, Lewis, what's the most you've lost in a game of chess?"

Lewis preferred not to answer. He looked certain to lose, but wanted to make the best of his last move.

"Say my name, Lewis," said the guest in a mocking tone of voice.

Lewis said nothing, making his last move, which seemed to make things worse. Instantly, the guest moved his knight and said, "Checkmate."

Lewis shrieked in a silent way, unable to breathe properly. I wanted to go in again, but he waved me off *again*, nervously—I gathered I had to stay away, or I wouldn't be safe from the cloaked man.

Lewis pulled the last drink to his mouth, which I later learned was poisonous—the kind of poison that strangely worked after the seventh sip— and gulped, glaring at the guest with a challenging stare.

"Don't worry," the guest said. "It won't hurt. You will be dead in seconds."

Lewis's face was reddening, and he appeared to be choking when he said, "I am sorry, Wonderlanders. I failed you."

"Don't be hard on yourself." The guest stood up and patted Lewis. "You were killed by Death himself. Like I said, I never lost a game of chess, not when my opponents played for their lives." His laughter escalated. "Of all those whom I appeared to and challenged with a game of chess, no one ever beat me; and I doubt anyone will. But to tell the truth, nothing feels as good as killing you."

"But you won't be able to kill her." Lewis clung to the edge of the table while on his knees, chess pieces rolling left and right on the floor. "I hid the pieces from my bones."

I shivered in place, watching my brother die, and listening to a man claiming to be Death itself.

And then the cloaked man turned and faced me.

In my mind I wanted to run, but my limbs were frozen. Even though he was an old man with a silly moustache, something inside me assured me that I was looking Death in the eyes.

"Don't worry." He brushed at his moustache. "I won't kill you. Your time hasn't come yet."

I stood speechless and paralysed with fear, clinging to the door's frame.

"But when it does, I will come for you." He craned his head closer. "And I will challenge you in a game of chess, and I will win." He laughed proudly again. "What? Did you think it was the Grim Reaper, some spooky guy with a scythe coming for you when your time comes?" He turned to face Lewis for one last time. "Rest in peace, Wonderland man," Death said. "As for Alice, I will settle for nothing less than watching her burn in an eternal hell."

Chapter 43

Tibet

The storm ends the minute I finish the last sentence from Lewis Carroll's sister's diary. Even so, I don't rise from underneath my coat yet. I'm not sure what I really read. The shock of reading this way outweighs the mystery of the storm.

Is the Chessmaster really Death? Then what does he want to protect himself from? And why does he want me to burn in hell?

And all aside, how can you kill Death?

My coat unfurls by itself, and I feel the sudden chill of cold outside. The world around me is an endless whiteout; I can't see anything before me. I prop myself up on my knees, and the storm snatches the notes away from my hands and swirls them upward. The notes are swallowed by the thickness of white, but I am not worried. I know what I've read, and have memorized it.

So the Chessmaster killed Lewis Carroll? If so, what's Carolus doing in this world? Why did Carolus even bother to fool me into killing him earlier? So many unanswered questions. The one thing that seems clear to me is that Wonderlanders—and maybe humans—die playing a last chess game against the unbeatable Chessmaster.

Is that really how people die? Does the Grim Reaper give them a last chance in a game of chess? Who'd have thought?

Out of the silence surrounding me, I suddenly hear heavy breathing, but can't see anything.

"Who's there?" I inquire.

I wonder if it's the Dude, that mysterious guardian of mine. Why does he do this, and who is he?

Suddenly a hand slithers out of the thickness of white snow. A gloved hand, covered in blood, stiffening like a predator's claws.

"Don't worry. I'm not Freddy Krueger from *Nightmare on Elm Street*." The Pillar pants, his head protruding out.

I let out a shattered laugh. "You're alive!"

"Of course I am alive." He coughs, crawling toward me on all fours. "In fact, I'm a caterpillar. I may not have turned into a butterfly yet."

My laugh splinters into tiny sighs when I see his face. What has the giant done to him? The Pillar is scarred on the cheeks and the forehead—the giant certainly pulled out that bald wig as well. There is a wild, thick slash underneath his neck, on his collarbone, which shows because his clothes are cut left and right, all but his white gloves on his hands.

I am speechless, feeling guilty. I should have helped him.

"I could use a hookah right now." He lays his head on my lap. "I'd smoke the pain away."

"You killed the giant?" I brush my hand through his hair.

"Ever seen *Fight Club*? It was the same down there. But yes, I killed the giant."

"You should have let me help."

"You're more important than me." He coughs a trail of blood on the white snow. "I'm just a nutty professor; Indiana Jones at best."

"Severus Snape, I'd say." I want to laugh but can't. "And what's with you and the movies today? I bet the monks never went to New York. It was you who taught them the American slang."

"You're too smart, Alice. It may kill you," he says with beady eyes.

"Did you ever notice ignorant and stupid people live happier—longer?"

"I did," I say. "Only they never live to have such adventurous lives as you and I. And hey, don't buy into this future thing. I'm not going to kill you, ever!"

"That's like saying I won't let Jesus be crucified if I go back in time," the Pillar says in his most morbidly sarcastic way. Who can blame a man so much in pain now? "I'm not afraid of dying."

"I won't kill you." I shake his head in my hands. "Do you hear me?"

"If you keep shaking my fragile head like that, you'll actually kill me now."

"I'm sorry." I pat him and stop it. "Why didn't you fight the giant back, Pillar? Why did you let him hit you so many times, for God's sake?"

"You mean 'for Todd's sake.'" He tries to wink, but his eyebrows are stiffened by his wounds. "I had to let the giant hit me so I could win."

"What kind of logic is that?"

"It's a known None Fu technique. It's called 'He Who Laughs Last.'"

"Never heard of it. And it doesn't make sense. He could have killed you before you had your last laugh."

"True, but you see, the idea is that the big troll was too strong, so I'd never have had a chance to fight him like a man, not even choke him with my hookah if I'd had it with me," he says. "The trick when fighting an unbeatable opponent is not to play their game."

"I'm not sure I get it." I use the edge of the coat's sleeve and dry some of his blood.

"In every war, there is one person reacting to the other, Alice," he says. "Like when a terrorist blows up a building. Suddenly he becomes the master of the game, because he sets the rules. Most people fall in that trap and play it his way."

"Which is the normal turn of events."

"No it's not. He who makes the rules of the game always wins—like the Chessmaster. So when the enemy enforces their rules, the one way out is not to abide by them."

"Are you saying you repeatedly told the giant to hit you so you'd become the one who makes the rules?"

"That's right. Instead of playing his game, I was now playing mine, with my rules."

"But he could have killed you."

"Common sense certainly endorses the idea, but no, not when he never knew why I asked him to hit me. Every time he hit me and I laughed at him and asked for more, he was puzzled, wondering what was really going on."

"And what was really going on, Pillar?"

"I was wearing him out."

"You must be joking."

"I'm not. Think of it. Giants like him kill with one stroke. It's their norm. Like most ruthless villains in this world, they're not used to a prolonged fight. All I had to do was to make sure I took minimal damage with each hit until he became frustrated with me. Bit by bit, his confidence in himself diminished, his perception of his giant self thinned, and he started to doubt himself just like any of us, because I didn't die or collapse—and took it to the chin and laughed. I was just a boxing bag with thick skin—or will—hit over and over again and smiling back at him. I was like all of us, any of us, suffering each day to make it through, and he, being a giant, had never seen such strength."

"But you could have been broken down any moment, before you'd managed to execute your plan."

"I have to admit the sudden storm helped a little. I think it's called 'faith.' That moment when you count on the universe to lend you a helping hand," he says. "Once I saw the look of doubt in his eyes, I hit back hard—and low. You know what really knocked him down? Not my physical power, but my taking him by surprise, and his own self-doubt. He couldn't believe I was still alive."

"What did you hit him with?"

"This." He shows me a sharp-edged computer motherboard. "Got it from the Deep Blue machine. It's pretty lethal at the edges."

It takes me a minute to let the Pillar's theory sink in. I guess it's his thing. I wouldn't be brave enough to practice it, not in a million years.

"Come on," I tell him. "It's time to leave this place."

"Got a ride?"

"A red hot air balloon somewhere behind the white snow."

"Whose is it?"

"The Dude—I mean the Red."

"Your guardian angel?" he says. "I'm starting to like him. I think he is in love with you."

"Oh, please. Why'd you say that?"

"He saved you twice in a couple of days. A Red is in love with you, Alice. I believe we'll see him again. Did he write you notes again?"

"Yes. He basically told me who the Chessmaster is."

The Pillar props himself up, unconcerned with the blood all over him. "I'm curious—who?"

"I'll tell you on the way to the balloon. Can you walk?"

"Not really. My left leg is numb. I'll crawl, or you'll have carry me."

"I'll carry you. I'll use my left leg. You can use your right, with your arm around my shoulder."

"A team." The Pillar's eyes brighten. "Could we get a McDonald's Filet-O-Fish with a badass Coke on the way?"

"We're in Tibet, Cao Pao Wong, so shut up." I elbow him playfully, while we stand and he puts his arms around me. "Is everything a joke to you?"

"If we didn't joke we'd die here. Look." He points at the bloody stripes on his white shirt underneath the torn blue jacket. "Always wanted a white shirt with bloody red stripes when I was a kid. I guess Stephen King's books really messed up my childhood."

Chapter 44

World Chess Championship, Moscow, Russia

The Chessmaster was losing it. All the news on TV showed a prime minister or president in every country looking for the Pillar and Alice. Even citizens in every country helped. But none could find them.

At this point, most of the world leaders were in their third or fourth move in the game—they were allowed to take their time with each move, so most of them stalled—and the Chessmaster was beginning to think he hadn't shown his deadly side yet.

He wasn't going to tell them he was Death, not now. He wasn't even going to tell them about his other few tricks in the bag, or why he was doing this. But he had to scare the world a bit more. In his opinion, people didn't fear what they were used to. For example, the world had been in chaos for years: the Iraq war, threats by ISIS, and all the bombings of civilians had become the norm to the public. It wasn't pushing them to the edge anymore, and he had to make a point.

"Swiss president!" the Chessmaster said, walking toward him.

"Yes?" Ralph Rollecks, the Swiss president, said in a pompous voice.

The Chessmaster eyed him for a while. He didn't like him. He didn't like the ten-thousand-euro suit; nor did he like the fancy cravat or the golden Rolex watch. As Death, he mostly enjoyed taking the lives of the incredibly rich and those who stole from the poor.

Not that every Swiss person was like that. In fact, the Chessmaster admired many Swiss scientists, artists, and even chess players. He'd met an incredibly supportive Swiss family in the past when he was still learning and mastering the game of chess.

But Ralph Rollecks was a sleaze, a thief, and a horrible man. He not only was president, but also controlled most of the Swiss banks—discreetly, of course. It wouldn't have disgusted the Chessmaster if these were the president's only sins, but there were more, many more.

Ralph Rollecks's family had laundered Nazi money after World War II through his banks, most of it still available to neo-Nazis in this very day. Blood money, which had been a byproduct of killing millions of innocent people worldwide.

"I see you have three moves left," the Chessmaster said.

"I do," said Ralph, adjusting his tie. "And I intend to take my time."

"No, you don't," the Chessmaster said, already moving one piece, a knight, in an L-shaped move.

Lo and behold, it was a neat and genius checkmate.

"Your queen's dead." The Chessmaster rubbed his mustache. "And so are you."

Ralph was furious, but there was nothing he could do. The Chessmaster's men were everywhere, and now he had to drink up and die.

"My death will not mean anything," Ralph argued. "My people will elect another president."

"No, they won't," the Chessmaster said. "Because once you die, something horrible will happen to Switzerland."

"What?" Ralph said, stalling.

The Chessmaster didn't answer him. He ordered his men to force Ralph to drink, and he did.

As Ralph weakened to his knees, uselessly untying his cravat, the Chessmaster looked back at the camera. "Now people of Switzerland will face a terrible fate. If you don't want your country to face the same fate, find Alice and the Pillar for me."

The Chessmaster laughed, staring at the monitor on the left, showing everyone in Switzerland falling asleep.

Chapter 45

Somewhere in Tibet

The Dude's balloon is a piece of art, which the Pillar figured out right away. True, it is red, but its hood is white, the color of snow, so when we fly it, no one will be able to track us with satellites from above.

"You know how to operate this thing?" I ask the Pillar. We are already flying.

"I think so," he says. "Saw it used in that movie *Around the World in Eighty Days*."

"That's all?"

"Don't worry, we'll get there."

"And where is that exactly?" I fold my arms.

"Kalmykia," he says, wiping blood off his cheeks.

"Kalmykia? Never heard of it."

"The Republic of Kalmykia, a federal subject of Russia," the Pillar explains. "It is the only region in Europe where Buddhism is practiced by the majority of the population."

"It's in Russia?"

"Yes, and bordering China. Very close from where we are. Got a nail shiner? I think I messed up my beautiful nails."

I roll my eyes, secretly admiring his sense of humor while soaking in blood. "What's in Kalmykia?"

"The next clue."

"The clue to the third chess piece, you mean? How do you know that? I haven't opened the rook chess piece yet," I say while attempting to pull it out of my pockets, only to realize the Pillar is holding it in his hands. "You took it?"

"Just before we escaped the monks."

"Why?"

"Needed to know what's inside."

"Did you open it?"

"Of course."

"And it said to go to Kalmykia?"

"No, it said to get the next piece from the giant down the hole." The Pillar furrows his brow.

I need a moment to grasp the fact that the Pillar is always a step or two ahead. "Are you telling me that's why you pushed us into the hole?"

He nods agreeably. "Or I could have simply run toward our plane and escaped. The monks hadn't destroyed it yet at that point."

"You knew there was a giant in the hole? I can't believe it."

"It was worth it," he says. "Because after I killed him, I found this in his cave." He shows me the third missing piece. I can't make out what it is with him gripping it.

"And that third piece says we've got to go Kalmykia?"

He nods, a wide, broad, and magnificently childish smile on his face. "A new adventure, baby." It's like he wasn't been hit to death a while ago. It's like he isn't in pain or dripping blood or has torn-up clothes. It's like we're not inside a ridiculous balloon in the middle of nowhere, racing against time to save the world. The Pillar is just happy we're going to Kalmykia.

"What's in Kalmykia, Pillar?"

"A most beautiful city, like you've never seen before." He raises his clenched hand in the air. "But first, guess what the piece in my hand is, Alice."

"Stop being childish. I'm not guessing. Just tell me."

"Come on, Alice. It's not like we don't have time to kill until we get there." He points at the vast nowhere we're flying above. "You know how many people have embarked on balloon trips and never found their way back down? Guess the piece in my hand."

I have to give it to him. He is full of life. He just doesn't care about our human worries. He lives every moment as if it's his last. I wonder if that's because he thinks I am going to kill him soon, or if that's just the Pillar.

"Okay," I say, finding myself giving in to his joyful spirit, and forgetting about all the blood on his hands. "It's a bishop."

"Wrong." He winks. "Guess one more time."

Chapter 46

Buckingham Palace, London

The Queen of Hearts hadn't put down the phone, still listening to Mr. Jay reading the Chessmaster's story to her. She hadn't heard a story that scary before. Who wanted to meet with Death face to face?

But the real question was: "What does Death want with us Wonderlanders, Mr. Jay?"

"That's what's puzzling me," he said.

"It surely has something to do with Alice," the Queen said. "He mentioned he wanted her to burn in hell."

"Alice never mentioned Death when she used to work for Black Chess."

"She was a wild one, Mr. Jay. She must have done something bad to him."

"To Death?" Mr. Jay sounded skeptical.

"What else could it be?" the Queen said. "Or why would he bother with killing the masses to get that Carroll's Knight?"

"I'd have to agree with you on this. Did you ever hear about those chess pieces Carroll carved out of his own bones?"

"Never before."

"Didn't Fabiola ever tell you?"

"No."

"Think harder." Mr. Jay's voice was demanding.

"I know you think she should have told me when we were younger and were still close, but no, she never did," the Queen said. "Besides, Carroll seems to have had her scatter the pieces all over the world, not long before his death. Fabiola and I were enemies by then."

"Then we have no choice but to let Alice and the Pillar find those pieces for the Chessmaster, and wait to see what comes out of it."

"I understand."

"We can't afford the Chessmaster slowing down our plans. He is on neither Black Chess's nor the Inklings' side. We just have to play along and get him out of the way."

"I think it's personal," the Queen suggested.

"Personal?"

"I am thinking the Chessmaster has a grudge toward Alice about something that happened in the past."

"Something that none of us knows about? It's puzzling me."

A long period of silence thickened the air in the Queen's room. She broke it by asking a question that had been puzzling her since she'd heard about the Chessmaster being Death. "Mr. Jay?"

"Yes?"

"I was wondering about this Death idea? I mean, I thought we Wonderlanders were immortal. We've lived over a century and half already."

"I know. And you're right. It suggests that most Wonderlanders are immortals, but it's not conclusive. In fact, if anyone had the power to kill them, it'd have been Lewis Carroll himself."

"But he couldn't. That's why he had us trapped in Wonderland. So how come Death killed Lewis?"

"Lewis was human, don't forget that."

"Are you saying the Chessmaster can't kill us Wonderlanders?" the

Queen said with a smug smile on her face.

"I think so…" Mr. Jay suddenly went silent.

The Queen could hear him conversing with someone nearby. He seemed to breathe heavier while listening. Finally, he returned to the Queen. "I think I just found the answer to your inquisition about the Chessmaster being incapable of killing Wonderlanders."

"And?"

"It's true. He can't kill Wonderlanders."

The Queen blew out a long sigh—and an accidental fart of mirth, though her dogs moaned in agony.

"Unless he finds the pieces," Mr. Jay continued.

The Queen stood erect, horrified by the implication. Did Mr. Jay really mean what she just understood? "Pardon me?"

"In order to kill a Wonderlander, the Chessmaster has to find the chess piece that represents that character in Lewis Carroll's chess squad."

"You mean the ones he made from his bones are magically connected to us?"

"I've just been told so," Mr. Jay said. "It seems that the Carroll chess pieces aren't of a normal character. They're chess pieces magically attuned to some of the most important Wonderlanders. If the Chessmaster gets them…"

"He can kill us, just like humans," the Queen said. "So the White Queen piece killed Fabiola because she was the White Queen in Wonderland?"

"Exactly."

"And the rook?"

"Margaret was the Duchess," Mr. Jay said. "She's always been your right hand. The 'rook' in the corner of the castle you're counting on. It protects you from harm."

"My God." The Queen collapsed on her chair. "The Duchess is the rook. That's why she's dead now."

"And I've been told something else," Mr. Jay said.

"What is it?" The Queen could sense the concern in his voice.

"I think you should run away, as far as you can."

"What? Why?"

"I've been told that Alice and the Pillar just found the third piece."

The Queen swallowed a lungful of her own fart right now. "Don't tell me it's a…"

"A queen. A chess piece of a black queen." Mr. Jay sounded disappointed. He definitely didn't want to lose the Queen of Hearts. She'd always been a great asset. "I'm thinking you and Fabiola had always been competitive. If she's the White Queen, then you surely are the Black Queen in Carroll's eyes."

There was a long silence in the room and on the line. Even the dogs went silent, waiting for Mr. Jay to spell it out.

"I think you're going to die within a few hours," Mr. Jay told the Queen of Hearts. "If not sooner."

Chapter 47

Somewhere in Tibet

"If you were a chess piece in Carroll's army, who'd you be?" the ever-playful Pillar asks me.

Now that I know the third piece is a black queen, and that the clue inside it was a yellow note that clearly pointed at Kalmykia, I have nothing to lose but to play along. "The queen, of course," I say jokingly.

"Queens and kings are lame," the Pillar says. "They stay back by the end of chessboard, hiding behind hordes of protective chess pieces, and do nothing but eat and get fat, just like in real life."

"Still, they're the most important pieces in the game. If you checkmate the king, the country will fall, just like in real life, by the way."

"It's a horrendously stupid idea, don't you think? Having one king or queen or president representing the masses."

"I agree. I mean, how could one man be everyone?" I say. "But you didn't tell me who you'd be in a chess game."

"I'll tell you in the end. I have a firm answer. It never changes. I am curious to know if you're like me."

"Okay." I shrug. "If not queen, I'd be a rook."

"Seriously?"

"It's a strong part of a castle. Essential, and it strikes me as brave."

"Rooks remind me of scapegoats," the Pillar says. "Just someone to take the blame."

"You have a point. How about bishops? They move diagonally in the chessboard and have no limits." I am trying to remember the little things I know about chess, as I am far from being good at it.

"Bishops are a joke," the Pillar says. "First of all, a bishop piece is an elephant. Why they ever called it a bishop escapes me."

"Hmm…haven't looked at it from that angle before."

"It's an elephant. Elephants are big and slow, so how is it supposed to have no limits? It's a flaw in the logic of the game, if you ask me."

"Then I have no choice but to become a pawn," I say, noticing I feel dizzy uttering the words. I wonder if I am remembering something. "Pawns stand brave, first in line. They fight like real men."

"Alice. Alice. Alice," the Pillar says. "You have no idea what you're talking about."

"What do you mean?"

"Pawns are nothing but the poor soldiers, pushed to the front line, defending our countries. They make movies about them and hail their names everywhere, but in reality, governments use them as sacrifices. It's the oldest trick in the book."

"Are you saying soldiers are useless?"

"Soldiers are the pride of our countries. We owe them our lives. They're the best humans with the best intentions, but they're manipulated, like pawns in a chess game. How many pawns did you see die in chess? Hell, how many idioms mention pawns in a sacrificial and humiliating sentence?"

I take a moment thinking about it. I hate to admit his point of view. I love soldiers who die for the freedom of their countries, but the Pillar's point is solid. Pawns are also used as puppets by government authorities.

"Still, don't underestimate pawns in chess games," I remind him. "If a pawn reaches the other side of the board, it can become any other chess piece. It's called promotion. I read it's one of the best tricks used to win a weak game using just one pawn."

The Pillar smiles again. "Nice touch. You've been practicing chess behind my back?"

"Just with a few Mushroomers back in the asylum. I don't think that counts."

"I wouldn't say so. Actually, the most prominent chess players in the world learn their best moves from homeless people."

"Really?"

"They're called Savants," the Pillar says. "It's a well-known fact. Savants live on the streets and usually are genius at chess, but they never realize they can make money out of it."

"So it's you who's been reading behind my back." I raise an eyebrow.

"Had to use my phone between the giant's punches. After all, you say the notes you read mentioned a final chess game that would mark the end of the world."

I let out a sigh. "So we're really collecting those pieces to play a final showdown against this Chessmaster?"

"It looks like it."

"Neither you and I can play chess, Pillar. We'll let the world down."

"I think the final chess game is rather metaphoric. Soon we'll arrive and see what's in store."

"So tell me. You said you have a favorite chess piece on the board," I say. "What is it?"

"Haven't you guessed yet?"

"I did. It's the knight. You love the knight, but why?"

The Pillar takes a moment, thinking it over, then says, "A knight moves in an L-shape, regardless of whoever stands in his way. A knight is a unique, unpredictable piece, and you will never see him coming."

I wonder if the Pillar is telling me something about himself. Something that I am not supposed to see coming.

Chapter 48

Tom Truckle didn't quite grasp Inspector Dormouse's visit. He stood behind his desk welcoming the sleepy detective, who'd just taken a long ride from London and still slept occasionally on the sofa in the room.

"Inspector Dormouse?" Tom Truckle said, shaking the man a little.

"Oomph." The inspector sprang up on the couch. "I guess I fell asleep again."

"You did," Tom said impatiently. "I am really wondering why you visited if you intend to sleep between every couple of words you utter."

"Can't ever sleep at home," Dormouse said. "Kids and their mother, not to mention the leaking tap that drips out of tempo."

"I can send you my plumber, if that will help," Tom said. "Now, if you don't have something useful to tell me, could you please just leave?"

"No," the inspector said, standing up and pulling his sleeves down. "You're the only one who can help me."

"Help you?" Tom walked back to his desk and sat. "What are you talking about?"

"I have important information that no one thinks is important, not even Margaret Kent."

"Then maybe it's not important."

"Of course it is." Inspector Dormouse yawned. "You will be interested, I'm sure."

"Why so sure?"

"My information concerns Carter Pillar."

Tom wasn't interested yet. Though he wanted to know more about the Pillar, he sometimes preferred not to. The professor had been a headache when he was in the asylum, and Tom still had nightmares about the Pillar escaping his cell without anyone seeing him. How did he do it?

"What exactly do you know about the Pillar?" he asked the inspector.

"I know why he killed the twelve people."

"Come on." Tom puffed. "Don't tell me the professor had a meticulously calculated reason to do this."

"It's stranger than you'd ever think." Inspector Dormouse sounded awake and alert. "Did you know that the twelve men had something in common?"

Tom tilted his neck, interested.

"The twelve men the Pillar killed were using fake names," Inspector Dormouse said.

Tom didn't see how that played out. It seemed strange, but not something that would interest him. "Fake names, you say?"

"All of them," the inspector said. "They changed their names sometime around the last five years."

"Are you saying they did it at the same time?"

"In the same year."

Tom itched his neck. The thought of popping another pill occurred to him, but he didn't. This seemed to go somewhere. "Is that all?"

"I wouldn't be here if it was." The inspector pulled out a long list of names and shoved it toward Tom. "This is a list with their names before they changed them."

Tom put on his glasses and began reading. Most of the names were foreign, not English, but that was all. "If there is a catch about this list, I'm not seeing it," he told the inspector.

"Of course you wouldn't," the inspector said. "Neither did I in the beginning."

Tom grimaced, his face knotting, waiting for the inspector's punch line, which didn't come. Instead, he watched the inspector yawn and fall asleep while standing.

"Inspector!" Tom rapped upon his desk, thinking about those pills again.

"Ah." The inspector woke, stretching like he'd been napping for an hour. "So where were we?"

"You said there is something special about the twelve men's names before they changed it. What is it?"

"All those foreign names on the list are a translation to one name in English," the Inspector said.

"One name?" Tom grimaced. "Are you saying the twelve people the Pillar killed shared one certain name—in different languages—then changed it to a fake one in the same year?"

The inspector nodded proudly.

"That's odd," Tom said. "Definitely interesting. But I don't see how this exposes the Pillar's reason for killing them."

"Not when you know of the name they all shared in the past."

"Is that relevant?"

"Most definitely."

"What is that name?" Tom asked, not expecting the inspector's answer.

It was such a strange answer that he had the inspector repeat it to make sure he'd heard it right the first time.

"Carter Pillar," the inspector said. "The twelve men shared the name of Carter Pillar."

Chapter 49

Close to Kalmykia region, Russia

"What are you doing?" I ask the Pillar, as our balloon floats closer to the ground.

He looks up from his phone, which he has been using to play chess for some time. "I'm playing chess against the computer."

"I see that," I say. "You've been clicking buttons like a child for half an hour now."

"I have the strongest thumbs." He grins, still staring at the screen.

"The weakest mind, too."

"Love you when you're nasty like that." He clicks a side button and plays a song, which has lyrics saying, *I'm feeling kinda mean... Blah, blah, blah.* "It's a song by Double Vision."

"So?"

"I need to feel mean and practice chess in case we're playing against the Chessmaster with Carroll's pieces."

"And a couple of computer games will make you good at it?"

"I am playing against the commercialized version of IBM's Deep Blue." He still grins like a child, making a move against the machine.

I'm beginning to get curious, peeking to see how far he went. "Any luck?"

"Nah," the Pillar says. "This is the seventh game I've lost in a row."

"In only a couple of moves, apparently." I point at the screen.

The Pillar glances toward me. "I think we'd better give in and let the world end. Neither of us can beat the Chessmaster."

"You've just said it may be another sort of chess game," I remind him. "Besides, there must be a point in collecting Carroll's pieces."

"Of course, but we don't know what it is."

"Maybe you can only beat the Chessmaster with Carroll's Knight. It'd make sense why Lewis scattered the pieces all around the world."

The Pillar seems to like the idea. "Not bad thinking for a mad girl who's a mere character in a children's book."

"Stop the joking. Be serious for a few minutes."

"Can I be seriously joking?" He raises an eyebrow.

"Stop it, really."

"Seriously mad?"

"Pillar!"

"I was thinking seriously funny. Now that's new."

"I'm not going to warn you again. Now tell me what's in Kalmykia. I'm sure the chess piece didn't say just to go there without further clues."

"You want to know what's in Kalmykia?"

"Yes."

"Chess City."

"Chess City? What is that?"

"A large complex devoted to chess competitions, located east of Elista, Kalmykia, in Russia." The Pillar tucks his phone into his battered pocket. "A small town, actually, with a domed Chess Hall."

"A center for playing chess, you mean?"

"Yes, but that's not Chess City's main attraction. The small city is an Olympic-style village of Californian-Mediterranean Revival Style architecture. It has a conference center, public swimming pool, and a museum of Kalmyk Buddhist art."

"And?" I tilt my head. Clearly nothing of what he's mentioned is what we're after.

"Chess City also has a complex feature of sculptures and artwork devoted to chess. One of them is a statue of a man called Ostap Bender."

"Who's that?"

"A fictional character of books written by Ilya Ilf and Yevgeni Petrov, Russian authors, equally infatuated with *Alice in Wonderland.*"

"What were their books about?"

"The character in their books proposed the creation of a world chess capital."

"That's interesting." I'm curious to see where the Chessmaster fits in.

"Earlier, Chess City had been used to host holy men like the Dalai Lama and such, but then, when completed in 1998, a millionaire from Kalmykia, ruler of the republic since 1993, Kirsan Ilyumzhinov, made this city into something much madder."

"I'm listening."

"Kirsan Ilyumzhinov was also president of FIDE, the international governing body of chess, at the time," the Pillar explains. "A fanatical chess enthusiast, and totally against the IBM scam with his friend Garry Kasparov, had the city expanded and built for the thirty-third Chess Olympiad."

I am not saying a word. The Pillar's story seems complex, so I keep listening eagerly, waiting for the punch line, because with the Pillar, there is always a punch line.

"Since then, Chess City has hosted three major FIDE tournaments. Kirsan Ilyumzhinov had future plans for hosting watersport and skiing events, but that never happened."

"Why?"

"You want the truth or the newspaper headlines at the time?"

"Start with the version told by the newspapers at the time."

"They claimed that due to Kalmykia being a poor republic of approximately three hundred thousand people located in the barren steppe regions in the southeastern corner of Europe, with scant natural resources, Kirsan Ilyumzhinov was corrupt and stealing the poor people's money," the Pillar says. "As a result, the construction of the opulent Chess City was abandoned."

"Abandoned?"

"It became a dead city," the Pillar says. "As beautiful as it was, the investigations never ended, and no one lived there anymore."

At this moment, the city starts to show itself beyond the fading white of snow in the distance. Slowly, I am absorbing the ridiculously beautiful and larger-than-life aspect of it. From this far, I can already see an endless chessboard built on the ground, much, much larger than the one in Marostica.

Beyond it, the rest of the city's buildings are colorful and enchantingly designed, reminding me of the ridiculousness of everything Lewis Carroll imagined in Wonderland.

"I can't believe how beautiful it is," I say. "How come such a place is abandoned?"

"Which brings us to what really happened with Kirsan Ilyumzhinov," the Pillar says.

"I'm curiouser and curiouser," I say.

"In reality, Kirsan Ilyumzhinov was a dear friend of…"

"Of whom?"

"The March Hare."

It takes me a second to connect the March to these events, but once I remind myself of the light bulb in the Hare's head, my brain lights up with the answer. "Are you telling me Kirsan Ilyumzhinov was searching for Wonderland?"

"Most definitely." The Pillar nods. "The March Hare, being chased by Black Chess, especially after they'd implanted a light bulb in his head, couldn't build more gardens to bring him back to Wonderland. Kirsan Ilyumzhinov, being a Lewis Carroll fan—so many Russians are, trust me, because of the time Lewis spent here—he persuaded the March Hare to build Chess City, which was supposed to be the next best thing to the Garden of Cosmic Speculation."

"A better model, you mean."

"The March had discovered that the way to Wonderland wasn't the gardens with ridiculous designs, but the secret was in designing a chess city from Lewis's lost designs in his diaries."

"So we're about to land on the real portal to Wonderland?" I say, my eyes fixed on the empty city.

"Not sure, but the city was banned by the Russian government—influenced by Black Chess, of course. There was no way to enter or visit it."

"Because they wanted to find a way to Wonderland," I mumble.

"Most probably," the Pillar says. "Though I'm not sure. What I know is that this place never worked as a portal to Wonderland, so it's stayed like this: a most beautiful ghost city."

I turn and look the Pillar in the eye. He looks back at me, impressed with what I am about to say. "An empty ghost town, which was once a possible portal to Wonderland," I say. "The perfect place for Fabiola to hide Carroll's Knight."

Chapter 50

The Queen's first way out was to hide under the sheets of her royal bed, but then the stupid dogs barked, exposing her hiding place.

She jumped out of bed, frantically wondering how she could cheat Death. If Alice and the Pillar had really found that last piece, she was going to die in a few hours, just like Fabiola and Margaret. How was it possible to cheat Death when your name appeared on his to-do list?

She kept thinking that Death could be bribable, just like anything else in the world. But what did Death need money for? It wasn't like he was in dire need of a new scythe from Harrods or ASDA.

Then what? She kept thinking.

What can I offer Death so he'll leave me alone?

She thought if she could talk to him face to face, she'd persuade him of something—or better, trick him into nearing her guards, and chop off his head.

Chopping off Death's head. She grinned. *That'd look good on my CV.*

But she knew she was just fooling herself. Death was coming. Soon she'd be poisoned and die. The real issue with Death was he didn't knock on doors. There wasn't enough time to offer him tea and talk him out of it.

The only solution was to fool him and make him think he was killing her when she was someone else. The Queen jumped toward the phone and called the Cheshire.

"I want you to possess me," she told him.

The Cheshire, or whoever he was possessing at that moment, was munching on popcorn and watching *The Exorcist*, which he thought was entirely rubbish. *If I was that terrible demon in the movie, why would I possess a helpless young girl? I'd possess the president of the United States or something.*

"Did you hear me?" the Queen said.

"I heard you, but I'm not sure I heard you right." He munched on more popcorn and turned off the movie to watch *Family Guy* instead. The Cheshire dug *Family Guy*. "Did you just say you want me to possess you?"

"Yes, that's an order."

"First of all, I don't take orders from you," he said. "You're too short to give orders."

"Cheshire! Possess me!" She stomped her feet.

The Cheshire almost choked, laughing. He imagined the girl in *The Exorcist* being bratty and all, demanding the demon possess her. That would be a great scene in *Family Guy*, he thought.

"Possess me!"

"You know I can't," he said. "You're a Wonderlander."

"Yes, you can if I give you permission."

"So you're serious about it. May I ask why?"

"Because…" The Queen had to cook up a reason, fast. She began to sob theatrically. "I'm fed up with myself. I'm short, obnoxious, and no one loves me. I can't think of one child who has me as his idol. I realized I'd prefer being a cat than a queen."

"What's wrong with cats?" The Cheshire purred.

"No, I didn't mean it like that. I meant I prefer to be a beautiful cat than being a nasty Queen who chops off heads."

The Cheshire gave it some thought. He'd been searching for a person to possess forever and stick with. Being the Queen of Hearts—and Britain's queen—wasn't bad, although he wouldn't want to stick to it forever. But it'd be fun, too. And he was seriously bored.

"Okay," he said. "I'm on my way."

"Thank you!" she chirped. "You have a pen and paper so you can write my address down?"

The Cheshire blew out a long sigh. "I know where you live. You're the Queen of England. Everyone knows where you live."

"Ah, stupid me." She blushed.

"I'm beginning to have second thoughts about possessing someone like you. So stupid, I could lose my cat mojo."

"No, no. I promise I'd buy someone's brain. How many IQs are good for you?"

The Cheshire simply hung up. It wasn't worth it, really. He switched the channel and watched *Dumb and Dumber*.

The Queen, on the other hand, was shocked, listening to the terrible beep of the phone. Had the Cheshire just given up on her? How was she going to cheat Death now?

She suddenly felt a shudder, followed by terrible cramps in her stomach. There was no escaping now.

She fell to her knees. Even her dogs abandoned her. She swirled and screamed and cursed and spat bubbles of stupidity out of her mouth. But nothing helped.

Fading away, she saw strange men wearing black armor and looking like the Chessmaster entering the room. They picked her up and began pulling her as her bones scraped the floor.

"Where are you taking me?" she said.

One of the knights laughed and said, "To the afterlife. Time to pay your debt."

Chapter 51

Chess City, Kalmykia, Russia

Walking through the ghost city, it was hard not to feel like a tourist, though admittedly a special one. The enormous chess pieces and constructions are dazzling, sometimes infused with Buddhist architecture; it's an almost ethereal experience.

"How do you like it in here?" the Pillar asks.

"It's incredible," I say. "But I have to admit, the city is also intimidating."

"Of course, because it's empty."

"So we're going to walk the city? Looking for Carroll's Knight?"

"I'm not sure. The clue didn't explain things further."

"I have an idea," I tell him. "With all due respect, all those beautiful designs are a camouflage."

"What do you mean?"

"I mean the city's main attraction is this." I point at the incredibly large chessboard, like the one in Marostica.

"I agree," the Pillar says. "But I also don't see how it could lead us to Carroll's Knight."

"Why?"

"Look, Alice. True, it's the largest chessboard I've ever seen, but it's empty, just like the city."

The Pillar is right. The chessboard is devoid of any chess pieces.

In silence, feeling mesmerized and intimidated at the same time, we reach the chessboard. The sun behind us is shimmering with a patch of orange flaring behind the cloudy skies. Surprisingly, there is no snow in Chess City, making me think the March Hare may have been right about it being a portal to Wonderland.

The chessboard is composed of huge tiles of black and white, like the one in the Vatican. The tiles are incredibly huge, and they could host four to five people, shoulder to shoulder.

"I think you owe me an explanation," I tell the Pillar, influenced by the images before me.

"What would that be?"

"How come I walked the white tiles on the Vatican's chessboard?"

"What do you mean? You're Alice, the only one who can save the world from Wonderland Monsters."

"That's the Alice you want me to be."

"This is the Alice you are. We're not going through this again."

"But we have to, because at some point I was the Bad Alice and I've worked for Black Chess. It doesn't make sense that I was able to walk the white chess tiles inside an important place like the Vatican. Did Fabiola manipulate it?"

"Of course she didn't," the Pillar says. "Fabiola helped you because she thought you were a nice girl who could save lives while being brainwashed by me. If she'd known it was really you, she'd have killed you."

"Then why did she show me the vision of the circus?"

"Either to make you realize Black Chess's madness, or she was testing you so she could, like I said, kill you if you were the Bad Alice."

"Some things you say about her make me wonder why you love her."

The Pillar shrugs. "I know. But hey, I'm as bad myself."

Sometimes I can't help it when I listen to him. I suppress a laugh and stay focused on what I need to know. "You still haven't told me how the Bad Alice was able to walk the white tiles in the Vatican."

"Because of your intentions."

"Excuse me?"

"We all have good and evil inside us. It comes and goes. Some of us dip our heads too far in the dark, and some only have snippets of bad thoughts clouding our heads from time to time. For instance, it may cross your mind to pull down the window and verbally abuse the reckless driver next to you in a rare episode of road rage. But it just subsides and you don't give in to it, once you remind yourself that being good is a choice, not a gene."

"Stop the metaphors. I need firm answers now."

"Because your intentions were good, Alice—that's why you walked the white tiles." The Pillar's voice is flat.

"If so, then I can walk the white tiles now as well," I say, taking a deep breath.

"You're assuming this is one of those holy chessboards?"

"It makes sense, since it's in a place that is supposedly a portal to Wonderland."

"A bit far-fetched," he says. "But if you truly believe so, then you should start with the black tiles. I mean, if you're right, my bet is you can't walk them."

"I can't," I say firmly. "I feel it."

The Pillar's eyes glimmer, not in the most pleasant way.

"I will walk the white tiles now," I say, and step onto the board.

The Pillar's first reaction is taking a couple of steps back. I believe he just read my mind and realized what I was aiming for.

"Now it's your turn," I dare him. "I want you to try to walk the white tiles, Pillar."

"Ah, there is no need to." He waves his hand, trying to act playful, but the concern in his eyes is exposing enough.

"I need you to," I insist. "I need to know about your intentions."

His eyes weaken. The shine in them withers a little. I've cornered him in a place he doesn't wish to be. But I need to know. I need to know, once and for all, what his intentions are.

"Don't worry," I say. "I will never kill you, not even if you can only walk the black tiles. All I want is to know you're on my side."

"I am on your side," the Pillar says.

"Actually, this is what I feel. I know what you've done to me. You believing in me is beyond remarkable. But there is this feeling about you I can't shake."

"What feeling?"

"That I don't know who you really are."

"I can't walk the tiles, Alice." The Pillar's voice scares me, because he is almost begging me, something I've never experienced with him. "I just can't."

"Are you saying you can only walk the black tiles?"

"I'm saying I can't."

I pull out a gun from my back pocket and point it at him. I confiscated it from the Chessmaster's men in Marostica and held on to it. I'm not even sure it's loaded, but I have to do this.

The Pillar says nothing. Somehow he is not surprised.

"I'm much more worried now," I say. "Why aren't you surprised I am pointing a gun at you? Is it that you don't believe I will pull the trigger?"

"Actually, I have no doubt you will, if you need to," he says. "And at some point you will pull the trigger and kill me. It's my fate, but I'm not sure why you will do it."

I grimace, realizing that maybe it's the Bad Alice in me aiming the gun at him. "I'm sorry." I lower the gun.

"No," the Pillar says. "Don't lower the gun. Don't repress that dark part inside you, Alice."

"What? Why would you tell me something like that?"

"Because this is why I helped you become who you are now," he says. "The world is full of good guys trying to fix it, always faltering when it's time to pull the trigger, because they have no bad side in them. You're not like them, Alice. You're perfect. A good person who was once bad. If you can only find the balance inside, you will save this world."

Like always, his words seep through, and I devour every syllable and meaning.

He is right. If I end up facing Death itself, I will have to pull the trigger. I can only defeat Death with the darker side of me. I grip my gun tighter and point it at the Pillar again.

"Then walk the tiles, Pillar," I demand. "Show me what your intentions are."

The Pillar nods, still reluctant, but he approaches the chessboard. And there he stands before a white tile, about to step onto it, but can he really do it?

Chapter 52

The Chessmaster listened to his informer telling him the latest news.

"The Queen is dying, too," the man told him.

The Chessmaster nodded, thinking. "And Alice? The Pillar?"

"They've found three pieces so far. In a few minutes I will be able to locate their final destination."

"I want to know as soon as they arrive," the Chessmaster said. "I hope the place is not far from here."

"It can't be," the man said. "The sequence of how they found the pieces makes perfect sense. The last piece was in Tibet, pretty close to us."

"Are you suggesting they're close?"

"They must be."

"Be sure, and soon," the Chessmaster said. "I'm counting on the accuracy of your information."

"But of course," the man said. "I wouldn't risk you killing me." He smiled feebly.

The Chessmaster didn't quite like being perceived as that scary Death figure. He hadn't always been that scary. He had a story of his own, a story that justified his actions—at least from his point of view.

But none of this meant it wasn't fun infusing much more chaos into the world. After all, with the powers he possessed he wasn't only capable of killing people. He could also make entire cities fall asleep.

He stood up, walked toward two other presidents, and with a couple of moves killed them, then simply announced more cities going to sleep. A slow, boring death, he liked to call it. *We all went to sleep—died every night—and woke up, never being appreciative of the gift of life.* Funny how this came from Death himself.

The Chessmaster announced the new sleeping cities on the news, warning of London being the next one on the list. Then he sat back, daydreaming about all the hell he would soon bestow on Alice. Oh, how long he'd waited for this to happen.

Chapter 53

Director's office, Radcliffe Asylum, Oxford

"The twelve men were called Carter Pillar?" Tom Truckle said.

"See?" Inspector Dormouse said. "I told you I know something."

"But what does it mean? Why would people named Carter Pillar change their name in the same year?"

"I have an idea, not much, but I am curious to know your theories."

"I don't know," Tom Truckle said. "Maybe they knew about him being a madman and didn't want to have anything to do with him."

"Sounds too far-fetched to me."

"Then maybe he made them change their names. I wouldn't dismiss the idea. The Pillar is a lunatic. I imagine his ego drove him to want only one man called by his name."

"It still makes no sense. He is a madman, and he fooled me by pretending to be some animal activist called the Petmaster, but it's not that," Dormouse said. "Want to hear what I know?"

"If you don't mind."

"The twelve men were foreigners. They weren't born in Britain, and none of them came from the same country."

"It's getting more interesting now. What else?"

"They come from all over the world, even from countries where you normally wouldn't find a name like Carter or Pillar."

"But you said their names were a translation to Carter Pillar in their own language."

"Indeed, but even some of those translations are never used as names in their countries."

"I see. So they arrived here a few years ago? Why?"

"For all kinds of reasons. None of them suspicious or unusual."

"That's a dead end," Tom Truckle said. "Did they know each other?"

"Now you're on the right track. They all met annually. Once every year."

"You don't say."

"A secret meeting, and guess where?"

"That's hard to guess."

"In Oxford University."

"Does that mean they knew the real Pillar?"

"In fact, yes," Inspector Dormouse said. "I had to dig into the university's archive to figure out that it was our Carter Pillar who arranged the secret meetings."

"What were they about?"

"Some kind of ritual."

"You've lost me. Ritual?"

"About Wonderland."

"That can't be."

"Oh, it can," Inspector Dormouse said. "I've bribed a cook who worked in the kitchen below Oxford to tell me all he knew about the meetings."

"And?"

"He heard them talk about Wonderland all the time. But the boy thought they were nuts. He was fooled by Carter Pillar pretending to be a nerdy professor at the time, so he dismissed the nonsensical talk, and only overheard a few things."

"Like what?"

"Like what they called their meetings."

"They had a name for a meeting?" Tom Truckle said. "I'm curious. What did they call it?"

"Are you ready for it?" Inspector Dormouse seemed too awake and alert now.

"Why wouldn't I?"

"Because I think it may tie a few things you already know together—in a vague way, though."

"I know you're a detective who likes suspense, but I'm not into that," Tom Truckle said. "So tell me what they called their meetings."

"I suggest you suck down a few pills first," Inspector Dormouse said. "You will need them."

"Damn it. Just spill it out. What did they call their meetings?"

"The Fourteen," Inspector Dormouse said, watching Tom Truckle pop down a few pills right away.

Chapter 54

Chess City, Kalmykia, Russia

The Pillar still hesitates at stepping onto the white tiles.

"Please," I say. "You owe me this."

His right foot is slightly higher, presumably ready to step onto the white tiles. I'm not sure if he is tricking me into playing one of his games, but he looks a bit thin-skinned at the moment. Something is showing through, but I can't quite see it.

"Like I said, I will not kill you, no matter what," I say. "I will not even hate you. It seems impossible to do so now, not after all we've been through, not after you've believed in me so much. But I need to know who you are."

"Beware of what you wish for," he says, almost mumbling it.

What's going on with him? Who is he, really? Having him standing in front of me, his clothing in tatters, blood dried on his bare skin in most places, makes him most vulnerable-looking now. This looks like a moment I can take advantage of. How many times do you get to have the upper hand over the infamous Carter Pillar?

"I am ready for anything," I say. "If you don't step onto the chessboard, I will assume you've been denied walking upon white tiles, just like you wouldn't do it in the Vatican. Fabiola may have been right. You're a devil in disguise." I raise a hand. "But even so, I will never blame you for it, because whatever makes you see something good in me, whatever makes you want me to save people, there must be a redeeming quality about you."

The Pillar says nothing. It's evident to me that he is sucking in whatever truth he is about to spill, right into the belly of his soul.

"There is nothing to be ashamed about," I continue. "I am like you. An evil girl. But I made a choice to be good and pay for my sins."

"Did you?"

I shrug. "I'm trying. Believe me, I am. I may not have remembered everything I've done in the past, but the basic principle is to try to be a better person in the now."

"I like the sound of that," he says, and steps further.

My heart races, watching his foot near the white tile. Is he really going to step on it? Knowing him, I'm sure he can come up with a last-minute trick.

In slow motion, holding my breath, I watch the Pillar step onto the white tile.

I can't believe it.

Even slower, he pulls his other leg up and now steps with both feet upon the tile.

I wait for something to happen. I wait for a trick. I wait for him to shiver and shudder in pain because he isn't supposed to be stepping on white tiles.

But all my assumptions are futile. The Pillar does have the power to step on white tiles. His intentions are clear, unless I don't truly believe in the chessboard's verdict. But I do believe in it. My heart tells me so.

"How is that for good intentions?" the Pillar says.

"Then why didn't you just do it?" I chortle, so happy. "Why did you play games with me? I get it. Fabiola wasn't right. You can walk the white tiles. You just want to come across as mysterious, like you always do."

"Maybe I have another reason."

I raise my eyes to meet his—they've been fixed on his legs all this time. "What do you mean?"

"Are you ready for this, Alice?"

"Ready for what? Please stop doing that. You're scaring me."

"You wanted to know my intentions, whether I can step on the white tiles or not. You wanted to know why I haven't stepped on the tiles in the Vatican, even when I can now step on white tiles. Scary or not, you asked for the truth."

It puzzles me what he is about to show me. What could possibly shatter this beautiful moment, knowing his intentions are "white"?

"This is why, Alice," he says, strolling over the corner of the white tile.

"What are you doing?" I ask.

"Showing you who I am," he says, and lifts up his right leg, leaning more to the right, then he stretches over to the adjoining black tile.

And there he shows me. It's confusing. Too confusing, in fact. But it's the truth.

The Pillar's right leg steps over onto the black tile. He can step on both.

I cup my shriek with both my hands, more bewildered than shocked, because I'm not quite sure what this implies, having both white and black intentions.

Suddenly, when I'm about to press him for an explanation, the whole life-sized chessboard hums in a low drone that I can feel in my feet.

The drone escalates to a rattle, which escalates to an earth-shattering sound, as if an earthquake is about to take place.

Chapter 55

"What's going on?"

"I have no idea," the Pillar says, stretching out his arms for balance, the same as me. "Hang on tight, Alice."

"This is ridiculous," I say. "We've ended up here because of the clue in the black queen chess piece. Are we going to die?"

"Unless Fabiola and Lewis intended a horrible fate for those who looked for Carroll's Knight, it couldn't be," the Pillar says. The whole Chess City starts to shake all around us. "Why would Lewis want us to die if he's scattered the pieces all over the world? He could have simply thrown them into the ocean for no one to find them."

"But he didn't." It's getting hard to keep balance. "He hid the pieces from the Chessmaster, but he wanted someone else to find them. Probably me."

It's this exact moment when I realize that the final chess game is definitely between me and the Chessmaster. Carroll's Knight isn't just something the Chessmaster needs, but also fears.

This is it!

This is the part I read in the notes, where it explains he is afraid of something. I think the Chessmaster is afraid of me. No, that's not quite it. He is afraid of me finding Carroll's Knight, but he also had no choice but have me look for it. Because whatever Carroll's Knight is for, Lewis was smart enough to hide it from the Chessmaster, and only have me find it.

My head spins as I think of my lock of hair, which released the very first piece in this journey. Lewis planned this all along. As always, he proves to be a genius.

A sudden, loud crackling sound rises in the distance.

It's like a microphone connected to the loudest of amplifiers. The crackling is too loud; it surpasses the sound of crashing and tumbling buildings all around us.

"What is that?" I ask the Pillar.

"Someone's idea of this being an excellent time for having a concert."

Someone's voice comes through the amplifiers: "By stepping on both white and black tiles, you have activated mankind's last game of chess."

The Pillar glares, with blame-filled eyes, toward me.

"I only asked you to step on the white tiles." I scowl.

"Yeah," he says. "It's always my fault."

The amplified voice laughs, ever so loud, as the shaking of the earth slowly subsides.

"Evil laugh," the Pillar says. "I'm sick of those silly laughs in Hollywood movies. I mean, what real badass villain laughs like that?"

"Me!" The answer echoes in the empty city.

I tilt my head upward, wondering if the voice comes from the sky, but it doesn't.

"Who are you?" I demand.

"They call me the Chessmaster," the voice answers. "My real name is Vozchik Stolb. But I'm sure the Pillar knows that already."

Chapter 56

"You know who he is?" I glare at the Pillar.

"I wouldn't have gone through this journey if I had, right?" the Pillar says. "He is trying to trick us for some reason."

"Am I?" the voice says. "But hey, my name isn't that important."

"Then what's important now?" I ask. "How could you have possibly arrived before us when it's you who sent us to find Carroll's Knight?"

"Believe me, dear Alice," the Chessmaster says, "it never crossed my mind that this, the Chess City, is where the final chess game would take place."

"Then why are you here?" I ask.

"I had you followed. It's that simple. Millions of people all around the world were scared I'd kill their leaders and put their countries into an eternal sleep, so everyone in the world was practically helping me," he explains. "Some reported seeing you in Tibet, a few spotted the poorly disguised balloon, and finally, a few residents in neighboring Kalmykia towns spotted you enter it."

"So you're as blind as us to where Carroll's Knight is in this city?" I ask.

"No quite that blind," the Chessmaster says. "Bear in mind that Lewis Carroll was something of a genius, having made the clues lead you here to a city that may also be a portal to Wonderland."

A light bulb suddenly flickers in my head. Is it possible that the March Hare knew about the whereabouts of Carroll's Knight all along? But that's impossible. I know he likes me and wouldn't keep such a thing from me. He is just a child inside a man, designing Wonderland-themed gardens and cities, wanting to go back to relive his childhood.

It was all Lewis's planning. But why?

"But you must have known something," the Pillar challenges him.

"Not until an hour ago, when I found out the clues led you here. I had my men search the empty city and found a few of Carroll's lost diaries."

"In this city?" I say. "What's in the diaries?"

"The diaries don't exactly point to where I can obtain Carroll's Knight, but they tell of a great secret."

"Spit it out!"

"It has to do with the chessboard you're standing on," the Chessmaster says.

"The one the Pillar accidentally activated," I remark.

"Nah, he didn't," the Chessmaster says. "That was a joke I made up. Nothing activates it, and the fake earthquake is part of the March Hare's nonsensical and absurd design, having planned Chess City to become another Wonderland. It's all done with the touch of the button."

"Never mind all that," the Pillar says. "What did you discover about the chessboard?"

"Ah, this will really amuse you." The Chessmaster laughs. "You see, each piece you found is connected to some of your beloved Wonderland characters. The white queen piece was connected to Fabiola, the rook to the Duchess, and the black queen to the Queen of Hearts."

"Is that why Fabiola was poisoned?" the Pillar asks.

"Exactly," the Chessmaster says. "At first, I thought this was how Lewis Carroll protected Wonderlanders from me. As Death, I've always been puzzled about my inability to kill Wonderlanders. Turns out Lewis protected most of you with a spell that demanded he created chess pieces from his bones and hide them all over the world."

The Pillar and I exchange glances. So this was why Lewis made that chessboard. It explains why the Chessmaster asked him about the chess pieces the day he took his life. Lewis really cared for the Wonderlanders, though he knew most of them were monsters.

"But I wasn't quite right," the Chessmaster says. "Each time both of you found a piece, a Wonderlander seemed to be dying, while in reality they were only poisoned, and some mysterious army of black men brought them to me."

"Not much of a difference," I remark, "because I assume you killed them when they arrived. My God, you killed Fabiola, the Duchess, and the Queen. Soon you will kill each of us, once you find the chess piece we're connected to."

I close my eyes, clench my teeth, and feel like I could kick myself for being so stupid. This is why the Queen was afraid of the Chessmaster. He is no Wonderlander. He is no Inkling. No Black Chess. But he is the one capable of ending the Wonderland Wars before they start, because he is about to kill us all right now.

Chapter 57

"You will kill us all!" I shout at the Chessmaster. "All you need is to find the rest of the chess pieces."

"Calm down, Alice," the Pillar says.

"I won't calm down." I am losing it, basically because of my stupidity. "He is going to kill us, and guess what? It's me who led him to the chess pieces by unlocking the tomb in Marostica."

"But he hasn't found the rest of the pieces yet," the Pillar reminds me. "And he doesn't know where they are."

"Yet," I retort.

"He is just a dumb old man with an ancient handlebar mustache," the Pillar argues. "He won't find the rest of the pieces if we just stop searching."

"Watch your mouth, Pillar." The Chessmaster's voice echoes. "I'm the greatest chess player in the history of mankind."

"Oh, please," the Pillar says. "Taking people's lives with a game of chess. You've destroyed my perception of Death already. Where is the cool dude with the scythe and skeleton for a head? Now that's what I call an awesome death. Chess game? Duh."

"Don't push me, Pillar, or I will tell Alice who you really are—and how we met before."

"You keep saying that," the Pillar says. "If you have something to tell her, do it now, you liar."

"Not now," the Chessmaster counters. "It's too soon. I want my masterpiece to be unveiled slowly. What good will it do me if I'm not entertained by my plan?"

"What plan?" I ask.

"The plan that will force you to find the rest of the pieces, Carroll's Knight included, for me." The Chessmaster seems sure of himself.

"You can't make me do it," I say dismissively.

"Don't ever threaten me, Alice of Wonderland." The Chessmaster laughs. It's a bitter laugh, tinted with sadness and outrageous anger. My curiosity about him increases by the minute. So he isn't just a mad chess player who wants to end the world, and not only Death itself. Then who is he really? Why is he doing this?

"Listen, mustache man," the Pillar says, checking his wristwatch. "Unless you have something really scary to show us, I'd like to leave and get myself some new clothes and a new haircut."

"Not funny, Pillar," says the Chessmaster. "Whatever you do, you will not be the 'He Who Laughs Last.'"

He Who Laughs Last? The words remind me of the Pillar's theory with the giant. I am beginning to think the Chessmaster was telling the truth about previously meeting the Pillar.

"As for you, little Alice," the Chessmaster says, "I hope you are ready to play."

"Play? You mean that last game of chess?"

"Indeed, but it's not like anything you've prepared for," the Chessmaster says.

His words are followed by another rattling and drone underneath the chessboard. This time, something else accompanies the sound. Not an earthquake, but an incredibly horrifying joke.

The tiles on the chessboard part and human-sized blocks of glass rise from under the earth. The whole thing is done with a most unimaginable technology. Slowly, I realize the chessboard is coming to life; each life-size piece of chess, black and white, is standing upon the chessboard, only they're trapped in glass prisons.

"What is going on?" My mouth hangs open.

I squint at the glass blocks and see that inside the large chess pieces are real humans. They're rapping on the glass from inside, panicked, just like me.

The glass blocks are foggy on the inside, so it's hard to see their faces. Out of nowhere, a block of glass rises and imprisons me as well, in the blink of an eye.

I start rapping on the glass from inside, wanting out, demanding to know what is going on. But a fog fills the glass and it gets harder to see.

I keep wiping it out with the back of my hand, realizing my screams are only echoed back in my head and are hardly audible outside.

But then, through a small oval shape I've managed to clear in the fogged glass, I see outside, and in that same instant, I glimpse at a few others who've managed to wipe clear a small opening through their glass blocks. It's shocking, and incredibly terrifying, when I recognize a few faces behind the glass.

In no particular order, I recognize three of them: Fabiola, the Duchess, and the Queen of Hearts.

Chapter 58

Aldate's St., Oxford

"This is no time to sleep again!" Tom Truckle pinched Inspector Dormouse awake.

Tom was in his car, driving to a place where he and Inspector Dormouse could further investigate the Fourteen Secret Society. They'd almost reached Oxford University when Dormouse fell asleep again.

"Wake up!" Tom's voice pitched up. The hectic traffic was already getting on his nerves. "What kind of inspector are you? A serial sleeper?"

"Oh, sorry." Dormouse brushed at his beady eyes, blinking heavily against the soon-to-set sun. "Where were we?"

"You said we should come to Oxford to meet someone who can help us with figuring out why the twelve men the Pillar killed had the same name."

"Yes, of course," Inspector Dormouse said. "I see you're about to park. Good. We should meet with that man soon."

"Just stay awake, please," Tom said, parking his car. "After we figure this out together, I have a suggestion for you."

"Suggestion?"

"Yes. I think you'd better retire from your job."

"Retire? And do what for a living?"

"A professional sleeper. I'm sure there is such a job in this mad world we live in." Tom pulled his keys out and popped a few pills. He was getting a bit drowsy himself, but he wasn't sure if it was the jinx from being with Dormouse or if he'd been swallowing too much medication lately. "So, let me think this over again. The Pillar killed twelve men whose original names were also Carter Pillar?"

"The same twelve men whom he had a meeting with every year. The Fourteen," Inspector Dormouse confirmed.

"So he basically knew these men for some time. Are you saying he played them, suddenly betrayed them, and killed them?"

"Maybe something came up and he had to do it. What's puzzling to me is why they all had the same name and then changed it."

"I know. It doesn't make sense at all," Tom said. "But if you ask me, I'm most puzzled by the name of their little secret society."

"The Fourteen?"

"Yes. Let alone the fact that this number always pops up in everything related to Wonderland, Alice had it scribbled on her wall. It's the date of Lewis Carroll's death."

"Could it be that the Pillar planned Carroll's death with the twelve men and then had to kill them? Of course, I'm just going along with what you told me about Wonderland being real—a bonkers idea, I must say."

"Wonderland is real. So are Wonderlanders. I'm one of them. You better believe it now or you'll pay the price for not believing, trust me," Tom said. "As for the Pillar having killed Lewis, it doesn't make sense. Why kill him almost one hundred and fifty years ago, then kill his accomplices now?"

"You're right about that." Inspector Dormouse followed Tom outside, heading toward the university. "So, back to my puzzlement. Why name the secret society the Fourteen when there were only thirteen attendants to the meeting—including the real Pillar, of course."

"Now you've got a point," Tom said, crossing the Tom Tower entrance. "So tell me why we're meeting that cook again?"

"He is the one I told you about. He used to eavesdrop on their meetings in the past," Dormouse said.

"But you said he knew very little."

"I managed to persuade him to tell me more."

"How so?"

"It turns out the cook we're about to see was a fan of the Muffin Man. Remember him, the cook from Wonderland whom Alice and Pillar killed some weeks ago?"

"I do. So you told him the Pillar killed his idol cook and now he wants to tell us what he heard exactly? I think I've underestimated you, Inspector Dormouse. You're brilliant."

"Only when awake." Dormouse nodded, looking flattered.

"We're all knuckleheads when we're asleep. Ever seen a brilliant sleeper?"

"That'd be me too," Dormouse said, about to smile broadly, but he stopped, staring at the scrawny cook waiting for them in the hallway with a kitchen knife in his hand.

"Is that him?" Tom said worriedly.

"Didn't I mention him being a former patient in your asylum?" Dormouse said. "You permitted his leave a few years back."

"On what basis?" Tom couldn't remember him, but he didn't usually remember any of the lunatics who entered, except Alice and the Pillar, of course.

"You mentioned he was a danger to the Mushroomers in your report." Dormouse shrugged. "And preferred that he live in the so-called sane world, rather than having him terrorizing your beloved mad people."

"Did I?" Tom raised an eyebrow.

"You did," the scrawny cook said. "I'm Chopper, by the way. Chopin the Chopper."

"Oh," Tom said. "Brilliant nickname."

"It's not a nickname." Chopin waved his hand in the air. "Ever heard of Frédéric Chopin, the French composer?"

"He was Polish."

"Whatever." Chopin tensed, his knuckles whitening around the knife. "His father was a cook like me. A cook who liked to chop. Chopin, you get it?"

"I got it the first time," Tom said.

"So, you want to know who the Fourteen really are or what?" Chopin said.

"I do." Tom nodded.

"Then follow me downstairs into Oxford's most underestimated kitchen." Chopin inclined his head in an unusual way, as if about to tell Tom a secret. "You know I've been secretly feeding Oxford's students cats instead of fish for the past five years?"

"Blimey," Tom said.

"Not any cats. Cheshire cats."

Tom swallowed hard, trying to remember if he'd eaten in the university.

"Why do you think Oxford's students are the smartest all over the world? 'Cheshire meat is all you neet.'"

"You mean 'need.'"

"Of course I meant 'need.' Had to change it, so it rhymes." Chopin's face went red. "Now follow me down the rabbit hole." He snickered, then itched his back with the kitchen knife.

Tom went to follow him, reluctantly, but first he had to wake up Inspector Dormouse from another sudden nap.

Chapter 59

Chess City, Kalmykia

I am astonished, staring at the three Wonderlanders behind the glass, among others I have never met. My attempts to break through the glass prove futile, so I stop, sensing that I will need my energy soon.

"You didn't expect that, did you?" The Chessmaster's voice attacks me from a hidden speaker inside the glass box.

"I'm confused why you didn't kill them," I say.

"Because Lewis's magic that connected them to their pieces didn't only allow me to kill them right away, but it gave me a chance to play with them the way I want."

It suddenly strikes me that all I had to do was throw the chess pieces away—or maybe return them back in place—in order to save them. By that, I mean saving Fabiola. Whether she wanted to kill me or not, I still like her and know she is one of us.

Margaret and the Queen I've never cared for.

"Pillar!" I call out, wondering if he can hear me. "Get rid of the pieces and save Fabiola!"

"Don't bother," the Chessmaster says. "I'm not counting the Pillar in this game. My men have already taken him to a place where he will be tortured equal to what he deserves. As for you, princess, we have a game to play."

"What do you mean?" I lower my voice—why, I'm not sure. It's like there is a suppressed memory that wants to break free all of a sudden.

"You don't remember, do you?" the Chessmaster sneers.

"Should I remember something?"

"Me and you, dear Alice. Me and you," he says. "But no hurry. It will all come to you. Besides, I love to torture you while you're still amnesic. Oh, the pain of not knowing, Alice. If you ever know how it cuts deep."

"Stop it! What do you want? Why have you saved Fabiola, the Queen, and the Duchess?"

"To use them against you," the Chessmaster says, and a sheath erupts out of the ground in my glass block. It peels off on its own, showing a sword inside. A hell of a long and heavy-looking sword. "Pick it up, Alice. You will need it."

For the first time, I don't doubt him. I pick it up to protect myself from whatever is about to happen. Boy, is it heavy.

"Now let me tell you about the rules of the game," the Chessmaster says. "Each of you Wonderlanders inside his or her glass box is taking their position in a chess game. The Queen of Hearts is the black queen. White queen is Fabiola. Margaret is the rook in the black army. I'd have preferred if more chess pieces were found, so we'd have one hell of a game, but maybe later."

"So, we're playing chess with real Wonderlanders in a life-sized chessboard? That's lame."

"Patience, dear Alice," the Chessmaster says. "It's not a game of chess, but a game of bloody chess."

"Meaning?" I ask, staring at the sword in my hand, all kinds of scenarios starting to play in my head.

"Black will play against white. When it's time for a piece to kill another, it will kill it, except this time, the killing will be real."

"How so?"

"You will see how," he says. "But you haven't asked me what your role in this game is, Alice."

"I see I'm in the position of a pawn." I remember the Pillar talking about how pawns are the soldiers sacrificed by their governments.

"Are you asking yourself why you're a pawn, Alice?" The Chessmaster's voice sends chills down my spine. "Because Lewis made you so. In the *Looking Glass* book he made you a pawn, wandering in a world of chess. How sneaky of him, making you the weakest piece in the game; the one that's on the frontline; the one that's like most citizens in most countries in the world, oblivious to what's really going on but also asked to defend their home country. Why Lewis betrayed you, you will have to ask him later…in the afterlife. Or maybe it's an after-Wonderland."

My neck hurts so much, and I feel like the weight of the world is on my shoulders. It's hard to escape the Chessmaster's logic. If Lewis loved me so much, why make me a pawn? Maybe he did it later, when I joined Black Chess. I must have done terrible things to deserve this.

"Lewis is a coward," the Chessmaster says. "You know why? Because a wise man once told the government, 'If you can't stand behind your soldiers who're defending your country, feel free to stand in front of them.'"

Now his laughter echoes against the sides of the glass box, its waves resonating back against me, buzzing me like shock therapy.

"I hope you're ready, Alice," he says, and my glass box moves forward on the board, two blocks, like in a normal game of chess. I'm the white pawn, and I make the call, kick-starting the game.

Behind the foggy glass, I catch a glimpse of the black pawn on the block parallel to mine making a move. Two steps forward as well.

I know what this means. It means my next move should be killing it with my sword.

"Do I have any control of my glass box?" I ask. "Can I open it on my own terms?"

"Of course," he says. "You just say 'check.'"

In a moment of utter heroic recklessness, I shout from the top of my lungs, "Check!"

The glass box slides down in an abrupt move, and I swing my sword to chop off the black pawn's head. But I may have been too slow, because a lot of blood splatters on the chessboard before me. Blood that could possibly be mine.

Chapter 60

The blood isn't mine. It's the black pawn's, whom I have just killed. His head rolls down his body onto the chessboard. It's the head of a man I don't know. A man who tried to kill me, and I had to kill instead. We've never met before, and will never meet again, unless it's in the pit in hell.

Suddenly, I realize how ugly war is.

"Don't bother if he kills us," Fabiola shouts from her block, her glass box suddenly open now. "He is using us—mainly me—to get to Carroll's Knight."

"How?" I shout, about to step out of my block to get closer to her.

"Don't try to leave your block," Fabiola shouts frantically. "It has an invisible electrical field that will fry you to death if you do!"

Her words catch me with the tips of my toes on the edge. I freeze in place and ask her, "How do you know that?"

"I designed it!" Fabiola says. "It lets you reach out your sword to kill your opponent, but never lets you out unless it's your turn in the game."

"Then what's the point of all this?" I ask.

Fabiola hesitates, readying her Vorpal sword. "He wants to trick you into winning the game."

"Trick me?"

"He is using you to win the battle on the chessboard because he knows you'll be willing to save me, and if you do win, something big happens, something he's been waiting for all these years."

"Let me guess," I say, "If I win, Carroll's Knight will be found?"

Fabiola nods.

"So give him the stupid knight, if it will save us!" The Queen of Hearts jumps up and down in her place upon the black block. Her glass box is open as well now. "Give him whatever he wants or he will kill us!"

"Shut up," Margaret yells at the Queen from her position at the far corner. "You short, little, stocky ball of evil."

"I will chop your head off when I survive this," the Queen warns Margaret.

"Stop it!" I yell. "Both of you! Maybe it's time we all stand on the same side, or we'll die and the Chessmaster will get his knight. And who knows what he can do with it?"

"Well said, Alice," the Queen says. "Why not start with you playing on the side you're supposed to?"

"What do you mean?"

"You're on the white tiles. You don't belong there. Stop pretending. The Pillar messed with your head," the Queen insists. "Come over, honey. Come join the Queen."

I find myself turning and looking at Fabiola. Her look is blank and I can't read it.

"What do you think, White Queen?" I ask her. "Do you still think I belong to the black side?"

"I don't have an idea who you really are anymore," Fabiola says. "All I'm sure of is that I *will* kill you if you cross over to the Queen of Hearts."

"Gosh, Fabiola." I sigh. "What made you so cruel? You're confusing me. One minute you urge me not to fall into the Chessmaster's trick, and the next you promise to kill me if I cross over."

"I've dedicated my life to this war, Alice," Fabiola says. "Sometimes I don't see people with emotion and hearts before me—all I see is black or white; Inklings or Black Chess. If you were my mother and joined Black Chess, I swear I would kill you."

"Don't cross over, Alice," Margaret says.

"Why do you say that?" I didn't expect that coming from her.

"It's a dark place where I stand now," Margaret says. "I have my reasons, but trust me, being on the dark side might grant you influence, fame, and so much money you could walk on it, but you will never sleep well at night."

"Then why don't you cross over, Margaret?" I ask.

"I'm so deep in the mud of corruption, there is no out for me," she says. "And though I urge you not to cross over, it doesn't mean I won't kill you if you do so."

"That's just amazing." I wave my hands up high, astonished by their logic. "Everyone seems to want to kill me today."

"Including me." The Chessmaster laughs in the speakers. "Now let's skip this clichéd pool of drama and have a good battle on the chessboard."

"What do you have in mind?" I ask.

"I will stop the electrical field now, and the white army will have to fight the black."

"That is crazy," I retort. "I might die. Fabiola might die, and then you will never get your knight."

"You will not die, Alice, not by the black army, and neither will Fabiola, and do you know why?" the Chessmaster asks. "Because you two come from the dark side. You know how to kill and win. You, Alice, are like the bravest of soldiers, a perfect pawn and killing machine. It will all come down to you. And once you win, the chessboard will reveal the whereabouts of Carroll's Knight."

"I know *I* come from the dark side," I tell him, "but Fabiola?"

The Chessmaster's laugh echoes louder. "You don't know, do you?"

"Know what?"

"Can't you see the tattoos on her arms?" he says, and I find myself glancing back at Fabiola. "You think those were from the days of her being a fierce warrior and White Queen in Wonderland?"

I turn to Fabiola with quizzical eyes.

"I'm like you," she tells me, sounding ashamed. "I was Black Chess once."

All hell freezes over in my head. It's impossible to even grasp what she just said.

"Why do you think I want to kill you?" she says. "Not just because of what you did back in Wonderland, or what you're still capable of doing, but because I fight the temptation every day. The temptation to return to Black Chess."

"That's so touching," the Chessmaster says. "This scene is better than any Hollywood movie I've watched, but hey, it's time for more blood spilling upon the chessboard."

And just like that, the electrical field is disabled. Fabiola runs toward me and we stand back to back, ready for the arriving army of black, led by the Queen of Hearts.

Chapter 61

Underground kitchen, Oxford University

"Here!" Chopin the Chopper handed Tom a kitchen knife. "Slice those carrots for me."

"Seriously?" Tom said, taking the knife.

"If you want valuable information then you have to help me," Chopin said. "Finish the carrots, then on to the onion. I will tell you what I know as we cook."

"I hate onions. They make me cry," Tom said.

"Wahhhh?" Chopin made a mocking baby face. "Do they make you cry, honey?"

Tom clenched his fists. "Why isn't Inspector Dormouse helping, then?"

"You sound like a child now," Chopin said. "The inspector falls asleep every couple of minutes. He could hurt himself. I did it once, see?" He showed his hand, which was missing a finger. "Chopped it off while working late at night one day because I was getting sleepy."

"Ouch." Tom stepped back from the missing finger. "What did you do with the finger?"

"Shoved it into the carrot soup. Looked like a paler carrot, but did the job," Chopin said. "Now, where do you want me to start with the Fourteen's story?"

"Why are they called the Fourteen?" Inspector Dormouse was alert enough to ask.

"Because there are fourteen members in their little circle of trust,"

Chopin said.

"I thought only the Pillar and twelve men attended," Tom said.

"First of all, the Pillar wasn't part of the fourteen members," Chopin said. "He was like the head of the community: taking care of their needs and organizing the meetings."

"Okay," Tom said. "Then according to you, there are still two members missing of the fourteen."

"Of course." Chopin chopped up some cucumbers fiercely, enjoying it too much, like a serial killer chopping off his victim's body parts. "Two members never showed up."

"How do you know about them then?" Inspector Dormouse asked.

"They talked about them. The Pillar, mostly. He had a great interest in finding the other two," Chopin said.

"Are you saying the twelve who were there weren't interested in finding the other two?"

"The twelve's main job in the meeting was to track the other two. Pillar's orders."

"So those meetings were organized to look for the missing two?" Tom asked.

"Part of it," Chopin said. "The twelve had some kind of deal previously arranged with the Pillar. Some kind of a grand plan that I will get into in a minute, because it's really bonkers. For now, let me tell you about who the other two were."

"I'm listening," Tom said. Inspector Dormouse was already snoring, and Tom wondered if the three of them were the worst bunch of men acting like detectives ever.

"One of the two was most important to the Pillar," Chopin said.

"From what I heard, the Pillar wasn't sure how to find the other."

"So tell me about the one he was sure of," Tom said.

"It's a well-known man. When I first heard his name, I accidentally peed in my soup—but shoved it down some minister's throat the next day," Chopin said. "Point is this man, number thirteen, was a man the Pillar couldn't bring to the meetings."

"Why?"

"Because he is such an evil man, protected by a tribe of criminals in a faraway country, and the Pillar seemed to fear him the most."

"The Pillar feared a man so much?" Tom asked.

"The thirteenth man was part of the Pillar deal," Chopin explained. "A bonkers deal I never understood. It had to do with something the fourteen men, plus the Pillar, did way back in a place called Wonderland."

"Wonderland?" Tom mopped his head in frustration, wondering about the many things that happened back then that he wasn't aware of. Maybe he was such a trivial being back then that no one but Lewis Carroll bothered talking to him.

"Wonderland is real?" Dormouse jumped awake.

"Just go back to sleep," Tom said, focusing on Chopin. "Do you happen to know what kind of deal that was?"

"All I understood is that fourteen men were involved with the Pillar, and that the deal wasn't complete. To complete it, the last two needed to be found."

"And killed," Tom said, assuming. "The Pillar was only playing those poor fourteen men. Whatever deal they had, he figured he had to kill them at some point." He paused for a moment and then said, "And that's why he hadn't killed the twelve for all those years since Wonderland. The twelve were his only way to find the missing two."

"Are you saying the Pillar didn't just kill twelve men, but fourteen?" Inspector Dormouse yawned, and Chopin seized the opportunity and shoved a tomato into his mouth.

Tom pried the tomato out, rolling his eyes at the silliness of his companions. "This is the only explanation. The Pillar only killed the twelve men when he was sure of the identities of the other two and how to get to them."

"You sound like Sherlock Holmes," Chopin said. "Though it should be Inspector Sherlock Dormouse who sounds like Holmes."

"Don't bother with Inspector Dormouse," Tom said. "We're getting closer to what happened to the Pillar. Now, tell me of the one person the Pillar identified of the missing two."

"You mean the thirteenth man the Pillar needed to kill, but was afraid of?" Chopin grinned, showing a silver tooth.

"Yes, him," Tom said, wondering if Chopin had managed to chop off his own tooth at some point.

"I hope you're ready for the surprise," Chopin said.

"Trust me, I've seen wonders," Tom said. "I'm hardly surprised these days."

"But you will," Chopin said. "Because the thirteenth member's name is the Executioner."

Tom was wrong. This did surprise him a great deal. "You mean the Columbian drug lord? The Pillar raided his crops and killed his army."

"The Pillar had to kill everyone in Mushroomland to make sure the Executioner, the thirteenth member, was dead," Chopin said. "Didn't I tell you I would surprise you?"

Then Chopin accidentally chopped off another finger.

Chapter 62

Chess City, Kalmykia

The shame of war was splattering on my face. With every head I chopped off or man I killed, blood covered me and Fabiola.

"I've got your back," Fabiola shouts, slicing left and right, her back sticking to mine. She told me this was the technique she used with her best warriors to kill their enemies in Wonderland.

"Am I supposed to feel safe with my back to the woman who promised to kill me?" I shout back, ready for my next attacker.

"Shut up and do what you do best, Alice," Fabiola says. "Kill."

Why does everyone think it's an honor to be talented at killing? If I turn out to have been the greatest gunslinger in Wonderland, I don't think I will feel proud about it. The idea of killing people you have never met before because they're wearing a different uniform baffles me.

But I have to defend myself.

"Why a pawn?" I shout back at Fabiola. We're still advancing, though most of the rest of our white army is dead now. However, Fabiola's strategy has worked so far. I have to admit, she is one fierce warrior. She even stabs her victims one more time after killing them, just to make sure.

"What pawn?" she says.

"Why did Lewis make me a pawn?" I slice another head off. "Why the weakest of the kingdom?"

"Pawns aren't the weakest," Fabiola says. "They're only underestimated."

"How so? I feel like a brainless killing machine you shoved onto the battlefield and, with my skills, I am only trained to do what you tell me."

"There is a wisdom behind that."

"What kind of wisdom, Fabiola? Please stop lying to me."

"Even though I don't want you to find Carroll's Knight, I was hoping you'd figure out the wisdom of being a pawn on your own."

"That's lame, White Queen. I might as well die before I have enough time to figure out anything."

"Behind you." Fabiola, in an amazing and unbelievable maneuver, moves to my side and stabs a black pawn who was about to kill me.

"Thanks," I say, frozen in place.

"Don't ever thank your soldier friends in war," she says.

"Why?"

She chops off the head of a black bishop who was about to finish me. "That's why, Alice."

I get the message and advance with fierce anger toward an approaching black pawn, slashing left and right, using my None Fu skills and jumping. Their heads roll off the chessboard, which is nothing but a red bloodbath now.

"Where are Margaret and the Queen?" I ask Fabiola.

"Don't bother looking for them. High governmental people are cowards. They're hiding somewhere," Fabiola says.

"Then how are we going to win?" I ask. "Aren't we supposed to kill them all, or are you still worried the Chessmaster will find Carroll's Knight if we win?"

"I'm worried, but we have no choice or both of us will die." Fabiola stands against my back again. "But winning doesn't mean having to kill them all."

"Then how are we going to win?"

"By you being a pawn?"

"What are you saying?"

"Search inside you, Alice. You must know the answer."

Instantly, I remember the Pillar being fed up with Hollywood movies. When Fabiola tells me this, I wonder the same. Why wouldn't she just tell me what to do to win? Why does she have to say things like "search inside you"? So clichéd.

But then, in the middle of my fried brain and torn muscles, killing left and right, an idea presents itself.

It's something I heard earlier. I believe it was the Pillar who pointed at it.

"I know what I have to do," I shout, advancing. "I'm a pawn. And if a pawn reaches the other side of the chessboard, they can exchange their piece for a king or queen or a stronger warrior."

"That's the Alice I've been looking for," Fabiola chirps.

"You mean the Alice the Pillar believes in," I say.

She pouts, but then lets it go. "Look, I designed this board to hide what's left of Carroll's chess pieces. You don't need to exchange pieces. All you have to do, as a pawn, is to make it to the other side and we win."

Even though I'm ready, I realize how much harder it is to advance than to fight in the same place. How am I going to kill all of them and reach the other side?

"Don't worry," Fabiola says. "I will help you reach the other side."

"How so?"

Immediately, she shouts from the top of her lungs, insulting the Queen of Hearts.

"Don't provoke me, Fabiola," I hear the Queen shout back. I can't see her, probably because of how short she is. "I will not die in this war because I'm too short. No chopping sword will find my head," she mocks Fabiola. "But I won't stand for you making fun of me! You know who I am, and what I could have done to you in all these years. You're only alive because I let you be."

"Then show me you can kill me," Fabiola shouts.

"What are you doing?" I yell at her. "She'll send the whole army to kill you."

"That's the point exactly." Fabiola smiles feebly, her eyes exposing her plan to me.

I get it. She is gathering the black army all around her so I can reach the other side of the chessboard.

"I'm risking the world for you, Alice," Fabiola says. "So make it count."

I am about to object, but the black army is already on her. Fabiola disappears behind several waves of black warriors, and although she gives me a last look before disappearing, I fail to comprehend it. What was she trying to tell me, other than that I have to reach the end of the chessboard and make it count?

Chapter 63

The Pillar's plane

Xian, the Tibetan monk, sat back in the fancy leather chair of the Pillar's plane. He was sipping a piña colada and looking at a *Playboy* magazine with eyes so open he might have fainted.

"This isn't what America is all about." The Pillar snatched the magazine from the monk's clenching hands. "I'm not getting you the visa to become a burden to the country. I want you as an asset. Most immigrants are."

"Sorry, Chao Pao Wong." Xian looked embarrassed. "I'm weak to Western temptations."

"There's no such thing as Western, or Eastern, temptations, Xian." The Pillar prepared his mini hookah as they flew away from Kalmykia. "This hookah is a temptation, if not an addiction, if you stuff it with certain ingredients, and it's definitely Eastern."

"What are you saying?"

"I'm saying you can be a monk, a donkey, or a good man wherever you go. It's your choice."

"So my American visa is a choice?"

"It is, but then everything is a choice." The Pillar smoked his hookah.

"Why so cryptic and gloomy, Cao Pao Wong? Is it Alice?"

The Pillar nodded, though he only made a slight move of his head.

"Then why leave her behind?"

"It's complicated, Xian. Sometimes we're forced to leave the people we love behind."

"I don't understand this. I mean, in the monastery we never leave a loved one behind."

"That's because there is snow surrounding your arses left and right," the Pillar said. "And because in this isolated community you're safe from life's everyday battles. Trust me, the visa will mess with your head more than give you peace of mind. You know why? Because it will force you to make choices."

"What's wrong with choices?"

"Well, for one, they seem like genius decisions at the time." The Pillar coughed, not happy with his smoke. "Only later, you may realize your choices were wrong."

"That's terrible."

"You know what's really terrible? Living with the consequences."

"But this doesn't explain why you left Alice behind."

"I'm not leaving her behind. She'll be all right."

"You truly believe she can reach the end of the chessboard and win?"

"She'll do that, trust me. She's a fabulous and fine young woman."

"Then what's worrying you?"

"The truth she is about to confront," the Pillar said. "Winning will only lead her to having to make another disastrous choice."

"Why am I sensing it has to do with her past?"

"It does. Alice will have to deal with a horrible thing she's done in her past."

"Don't we all do that all the time?"

"You have no past, snowbird, so pull yourself out of it." The Pillar tensed. "Alice is about to choose the Inklings or Black Chess."

"I have the feeling she will choose the Inklings."

"Me too, but I wish it was that easy. Because if you ask any person about the truth, they'd tell you it's either black or white…"

"Inklings or Black Chess," Xian said. "It makes sense."

"You're wrong, Xian. The truth is never black or white. That's the Hollywood perspective."

"Then what is the color of truth?"

"Grey," the Pillar said. "An ugly grey that makes London's rainy and creepy afternoons look like heaven in greens."

Chapter 64

Chess City, Kalmykia

Every step in my journey to the end of the chessboard reminds me of my cowardice. How can I let Fabiola die? This logic of war and how it's supposed to be dealt with confuses me again. I'll be saying it again and again. War is just an ugly and blinding grey.

A couple of black army soldiers notice my escape and return to attack me, but I handle them with swift ease. The smell of blood on me is not only nauseating, but humiliating as well. I hate having killed all of them.

Behind me, I can still hear Fabiola yelling as she is killing them left and right. What a fabulous and admirable warrior. But I'm almost aware of hearing her scream in pain twice. She's been stabbed, badly, but she will not give up until they steal her last breath.

And here I am, one step away from the last tile. There is no one to stop me but the short and stocky Queen, yelling at her guards. But none of them are here now. Fabiola has taken their attention.

I step on the last white tile at the end, and suddenly it all stops. All the soldiers turn and face me, though I can't see Fabiola, who is probably lying dead on the floor behind them. The horror on the Queen's face is worth a nomination for Instagram's pic of the year.

It puzzles me how stupid the Queen is. I mean, reaching the end of the chessboard will show the Chessmaster the whereabouts of Carroll's Knight, and he will not feel the need to kill the Queen of Hearts anymore.

But, being stubborn and war hungry, she can't understand now. Once blood was spilling on the floor, she could see nothing but war in her mind. Maybe the Chessmaster is right about trying to kill the likes of her.

After a few moments of silence, as I'm catching my breath and calming down, we start hearing a rattling sound on the square assigned to the white knight on the life-size chessboard.

Another glass box rises out of it. This one opens from the top. It's more like a podium with a prize upon it.

A chessboard with white and black chess pieces is stacked upon its surface. These are the pieces carved from Carroll's bones. This is what the Chessmaster killed so many people for.

I wonder if it's worth it.

The Chessmaster's men arrive and signal for the white and black armies to leave. He doesn't care about the Queen or Margaret anymore. In the distance, I see Fabiola silently sprawled on the ground.

"So this is what I've been waiting for." The Chessmaster arrives finally, guarded by his men.

He approaches the podium with care and checks the chess pieces one by one. He even sniffs them with a euphoric feeling I've never seen before.

"I told you I will find your bones, Lewis," he whispers to them, but it doesn't take a genius to read his lips.

"So that's what you wanted?" I ask.

"It certainly and most delightedly is," he says. "You know all the pieces are on this chessboard? It means that the pieces you've collected were fakes. Fabiola certainly cooked up a brilliant plan to hide Carroll's bones. I mean, all this hocus pocus about the chess pieces being scattered all over the world and hiring the likes of Father Williams was one big distraction to the location of the real pieces. And look where she's hidden them? In the Chess City that once was thought to be a portal to Wonderland." He snickers, eyes fixed on me. "You remember Wonderland, Alice, don't you?"

"Hardly."

"But you must remember it," he says. "And if you don't, trust me, I will remind you."

"Let's stop the talking. You got what you wanted. Release the world's leaders and wake the cities that are sleeping. I have no intention of getting to know you better."

"But you will know me better." The Chessmaster places both hands behind his back and approaches me. "In fact, one day not so long ago, you knew me very well."

"I don't remember you."

"But I will remind you of who I am, and what you have done to me."

"So this is personal?" I shrug. "I hurt you when were in Wonderland? Why would I regret hurting a monster like you?"

"You want to know why?" The Chessmaster's breath is on my face. "Because I wasn't a monster then. It was you who was a monster, Alice of Black Chess."

Chapter 65

Underground kitchen, Oxford University

"So the Pillar killing the Executioner was a hoax?" Inspector Dormouse asked.

"Probably," Tom said. "He made the world think he was freeing them from the worst drug empire in the world, while executing his brilliant plan."

"What plan?" Inspector Dormouse asked. "We don't even know why he killed the thirteen—or fourteen—men."

"A deal that went awry, that's all we need to know," Tom said. "What matters is that it had nothing to do with saving the world or Alice being the Real Alice."

"I heard a few members talking about this when the Pillar hadn't arrived yet in one of the meetings," Chopin said. "They argued that he used Alice to kill the Executioner for him. They believed Alice had certain powers or secrets that helped him do it."

"Doesn't matter," Tom said. "The man is pure evil. He has the capacity and slyness to fool the world and come out with no blood on his gloves."

"Still, I need to know what this is all about," Inspector Dormouse said. "Fourteen people making a deal with the devil, in our case the Pillar, and then being killed years later by him. Why? Did they break the deal? Did he deceive them?"

"Hard to tell, inspector," Tom said. "Also, none of this tells us who the Pillar really is."

"Maybe we will never find out," Inspector Dormouse said. "Chopin, anything else? How about the fourteenth member?"

"It's hard to tell," Chopin said. "All I know is that the Pillar couldn't find him."

"Any reason why?"

"I overheard the Fourteen mention that the fourteenth member was so sly he managed to hide his identity from all of them," Chopin said. "Meaning, he changed his name and escaped before the time they'd previously agreed upon."

"So changing their names was part of the deal?" Tom asked.

"Don't you get it?" Dormouse said. "This whole deal was about the Fourteen keeping the secret and changing their names at a certain time so the secret dies with them, except that the Pillar broke this deal and, for some reason, had to get rid of them."

"Probably because he sensed they'd expose him," Tom said. "But what in God's name was the deal?"

"I think I know," Chopin said, putting the knife down, looking agitated. "Look, I'm not sure I heard this right, but since you seem to be stuck, I have to tell you."

"Speak up," Tom demanded.

Chopin minded the wound on his newly chopped finger, making sure he wasn't bleeding anymore, and tucked his lost finger into his pocket—for a later carrot soup, probably. "I don't believe in magic or spirits or all these things, but here is what I once overheard."

"Just say it," Tom said.

"I heard the Fourteen once joke that they sold their souls to the devil."

Chapter 66

Chess City, Kalmykia

The Chessmaster's men usher me toward a building decorated in Buddhist ornaments and architecture. It's one of the most memorable buildings in Chess City. No one says a word to me.

Inside, a few Tibetan women help me take a bath and put on better, cleaner clothes. They take care of my nails and hair, but they don't speak my language, so I don't know what's going on.

I have no choice but to go along, since the Chessmaster, though having found what he wanted, has refused to release the world leaders.

"You and I, Alice, we have one last chess game to play." These were his words. "I want you to look good for the end of either your life or mine."

One of the women brings me a chessboard, books about chess, and DVDs about the Chessmaster's previous games. This one, unlike the others, speaks English.

"Why those?" I ask.

"You need to prepare yourself," she says. "The Chessmaster has never lost a game. He even won the game with…"

"God, I know, and I don't care about all of this propaganda. I don't have any idea how to play chess."

"Then you will die." She grins happily.

"Is he seriously intent on playing a final chess game with me?" I ask. "A real game of chess? I thought it was a metaphor."

"The Chessmaster loves chess. It's his life, and just so you know, there is a prophecy about you and him playing the last chess game in the world."

"I know about the stupid prophecy. I read it in some ancient note," I say. "But this is ridiculous. He knows I will lose."

"If you lose, people will die, and the world will end, too."

"Thanks for reminding me." I cough, almost chortling. "Are you saying I'm playing that same game he killed the Pope with?"

"And all the other world leaders," she remarks. "He has killed a few more in the last few hours and put more cities to sleep. They say Oxford and London will be put to sleep next."

"I have to see the Chessmaster and talk to him. He needs to know I can't play chess. Whatever happened between us in the past, there must be another way to solve it."

"No other way. Win or lose," she says. "Remember, after every move, you drink a small cup of poison. The poison makes you dizzy and doesn't kill you until your seventh move. If you can't beat the Chessmaster before this one, you will die. Thank you very much."

Chapter 67

The last chess game, Chess City, Kalmykia

The auditorium they send me to has bright lights, almost blinding, focused on two chairs with a table in the middle and a chessboard upon it. Carroll's chessboard, with pieces made of his bones.

Walking onto the stage, I hear murmurs and heavy breathing from the audience, but it's too dark to see them. This intimidates me even more.

I'm asked to sit on my chair, creepily tagged with the words *Alice: Loser*.

It looks like a gravestone, not a chair to sit on and play chess. But I have no choice and take my place.

In front of me, I realize I will be playing with the black pieces. The Chessmaster with the white. I'm not sure what's going on.

Why is the Chessmaster playing with white chess pieces?

Then my eyes catch a strange sight. One of the white pieces, specifically the knight, is missing. It's the only piece that's missing on the whole board. I'm assuming this is where Carroll's Knight is supposed to be.

But I am not catching the meaning behind it.

On both sides of the chessboard I see seven small cups, filled with that poison the Tibetan woman mentioned. I swallow hard. Will I really drink seven cups and die today?

A few tight breaths later, the unseen crowd applauds. Cocking my head, I see the Chessmaster arrive.

He strolls over as if he were Julius Caesar. Brushes his handlebar mustache to the left and right. Even combs the thin hairs on his head, and bows to the invisible crowd in his ridiculous armor outfit.

Suddenly, it strikes me. His outfit is that of a knight. So is he actually Carroll's Knight? I don't get it.

The Chessmaster sits with ease and then lightly touches the top of each of his chess pieces for luck, or as some kind of ritual. He doesn't meet my eyes, but then pulls out a chess piece of a white knight, rubs it gently with his hands and kisses it, then places it on the board where it should be.

"My beloved white knight," he says. "Carroll's Knight."

"Congratulations. I figured." I keep an expressionless face.

"This is what you, Alice, helped me retrieve after all these years."

"I wonder why it's so important."

"I can't win without it," he says with a smile. It's the smile of a psychopath, but it's strangely genuine.

"I find that hard to believe," I say. "You've never lost a game, and yet you were playing without it."

"Smart girl." He claps his hands, the flesh barely meeting, like an aristocratic old lady living in an ancient mansion she's never left for ages. "That I will answer, but first I need you to listen to this."

He claps once more and the speakers start playing a nonsensical song. It's all vocals of children and has no music in it. Probably some sort of a poem. I realize it's called "Haddock's Eyes."

"Remember this one, Alice?" He tilts his head with curiosity.

I do. "It's a poem in *Alice Through the Looking Glass*."

"Bravo." He claps. "Clever girl. Does it remind you of me?"

"I don't know who you are."

"But you do know me. You used to know my children, too. My wife and my grandmother."

"We were neighbors in Wonderland?"

"Not exactly." He raises a single forefinger. "But back to your question: why I can't win without Carroll's Knight?"

"I'm all ears."

His eyes dim, and a dark flash of anger and a vengeance-seeking look consumes me in ways I can't explain. I feel sucked in by his stare, watching him lean forward. "Because Carroll denied me taking my revenge on you and killing you, though he knew what you did to me." His voice is really unsettling. Not because he is scary, but because he is sincere. A sincere villain isn't a good thing.

"I get it that I hurt you in Wonderland. You still haven't explained the necessity of Carroll's Knight."

"It's the only piece in chess I can kill you with, and I have it now. And the irony? You brought it to me. The double irony? That Lewis made Fabiola bury and hide it in Chess City." His eyes are moistening, and it's getting to me. "And triple irony? That Lewis made the chess piece I can kill you with in the first place. I guess he was confused about whether to kill you or give you another chance, so he left it to Fabiola, and the random fate of finding Carroll's Knight."

There is too much for me to absorb here, but what is most troubling is the Chessmaster's ability to make me feel evil.

"You can't win this game, Alice. I've mastered the game of chess for almost two centuries, so I will never lose one," he says. "You know why? Because I was waiting for this moment all my life. You deserve this, Alice. To burn in hell. And all I needed was Carroll's Knight."

He pats his beloved chess piece one more time, as if it were alive.

So many questions are on my mind. What could I have possibly done in the past to this man that made him hate me so much? But the one that comes out of my mouth is this: "Why a knight? Why not any other piece?"

"Because I, the Chessmaster, Vozchik Stolb, was a Wonderlander once," he says in a tone so friendly and naive that I'm starting to hate myself for hurting him. "In fact, I was the funniest, most harmless, of Wonderlanders. Lewis has mentioned me with care and I'm proud of it—though I still hate him."

"Mentions you in the book?" I ask. "Who are you?"

"I'm the White Knight."

Chapter 68

"Devil, my arse," Tom snapped. "You don't expect me to believe that?"

"Why not?" Inspector Dormouse said. "You believe in the nonsense of Wonderland and not in good and evil and the forces beyond our grasp."

"Everything is beyond your grasp, inspector," Tom said. "You're asleep two-thirds of your life. I'm surprised you know what it's like to be awake."

Chopin snickered.

"So you think the Pillar is the devil?" Inspector Dormouse turned his gaze toward the cook.

"I didn't say that." Chopin shrugged. "But look, I accidentally chop off a finger every time I mention the Pillar. Diabolic!"

"You heard anything else?" Dormouse said. "Please remember. It's important."

"I don't want to remember." Chopin pulled his chin up and away, like a silly cartoon character in a manga. "I only have eight fingers left."

"How about a hundred pounds?" Inspector Dormouse slapped the money on the kitchen table.

"For a finger?" Chopin seemed interested.

"Two hundred pounds." Dormouse pulled out another hundred.

"I need three hundred pounds," Chopin said.

"Why? You've lost only two fingers." Tom felt the need to interfere.

"And I will lose a third once I mention that devil again," Chopin said.

"Here is another hundred." Tom offered a hundred of his own, not sure why he felt so curious all of a sudden. Maybe he'd like to see Chopin lose another finger.

"Talk!" Dormouse seemed aggressive.

"Say what?" Chopin said. "I will not talk."

"But you took the money," Tom argued.

"I didn't say I would not fulfill my promise, but I will not talk."

"You're wasting our time," Dormouse said.

"No I'm not." Chopin pulled a flash drive from his pocket. "This will tell you what you need to know."

"What is this?" Tom squinted at the drive suspiciously. "A bomb?"

"Why would I explode myself with you losers?" Chopin said. "This is a secret recording of some of the sessions. You go over it and hear everything."

"Why haven't you told us about this before?" Tom snapped.

"And lose three hundred pounds?" Chopin said.

"But you also lost a finger." Tom was getting mad.

"The devil took one finger, yes, but I fooled the devil and kept the other when you gave me the last hundred *and* I didn't talk." Chopin looked sideways, as if the devil were hiding in a teapot nearby, listening to his genius conspiracy.

"Give it to me." Tom snatched the drive, but then something incredibly unexpected happened.

Dormouse found himself standing in a room where both Chopin and Tom fell asleep while standing on their feet. It didn't take him long to realize it was the Chessmaster's doing. The madman had earlier announced that he'd make Oxford and London sleep next.

"Hmm…" Inspector Dormouse picked up the flash drive, wondering why he was the only one left awake. "This is weird."

He took the flash drive outside, preparing to listen to it in Tom's car stereo—it had an MP3 player that would accept the flash drive—and looked around at a sleeping University of Oxford.

"I don't think it's weird," he said. "I think it's frabjous. The one man who sleeps the most is the only one awake right now. Could it be that my sleeping has kept me immune to the Chessmaster's curse?"

Chapter 69

The last chess game, Chess City, Kalmykia

"The White Knight?" I say, unable to fathom this.

In the books, the White Knight was the gentlest and most beloved creature in Wonderland. In spite of his short appearance, he saved Alice from his opponent, the Red Knight. I remember reading about him repeatedly falling off his horse and landing on his head. He also had those silly inventions: pudding with ingredients like blotting paper, an upside-down container, and anklets to guard his horse against shark bites.

How could this good man have become who he is now?

"I see you remember me now," the Chessmaster says.

"I remember what I read in the book about you," I say. "That's all."

"It will come to you," he says. "All the things you've done to me."

"Why not remind me?"

"I'm afraid if I do, you'll die from shock before I can beat you in the game."

"If so, you should have just told me long ago and refrained from finding Carroll's Knight," I say. "Stop playing games. Tell me what I did. I'm very curious how I ever managed to hurt Death."

"That's the thing, Alice," he says. "I never was Death before what you did to me."

This is a complicated thing. Did I create Death in the past?

"I didn't even ask to become Death."

"Now I'm starting to doubt your story. It'd make more sense if you longed to become Death to have your revenge. I'd believe that."

"Not if there had been a ritual involved." His words echo in the back of my head, and suddenly I feel dizzy again, as if I'm about to remember.

"Ritual?"

"The unholy ritual that made you kill my daughter."

My hand reaches for the edge of the table and grabs on to it. More dizziness. Faint memories, blurred by older sins. "I killed your daughter?"

"Two, actually." The Chessmaster genuinely exposes his pain, and it cuts through and splinters my whole being into ripped pieces.

I have nothing to say, except to wish this hadn't happened.

"And my wife," the Chessmaster recounts. "My grandmother and my farm dog."

"I did that?"

"It's not easy realizing you were the villain, is it, Alice?" The Chessmaster's anger is now surfacing. All the fluff is starting to wear off and the demon of vengeance is rising. "Villains are so misunderstood. People see them killing and raging, but they never ask themselves why they've become what they've become."

"I'm not a villain."

"All villains say that, even in movies." He smirks, pulling one side of his mustache.

"I'm really sorry if I've done any of that, but you must understand that I've—"

"Changed?" He tilts his head and places a hand behind his ear. "You realize this is every villain's poor excuse when they're about to hang him?"

"You have to believe me," I plead, ready to get on my knees and ask for forgiveness, even ready to pay for my wrongdoing. I just need him to understand that I'm not the same person anymore, that I don't even know who that person is. "There are no words that could ease your pain. It's so horrible what I've done. Believe me. Please, believe me when I tell you I don't remember any of it. I don't even have an idea why I did it."

"Oh, please." The Chessmaster jolts the table as he stands, scattering all the pieces, all but his white knight. It stands firmly in place, unaffected by whatever wants to move it. "You know why you did it. Because of the ritual."

"The ritual again? What ritual?"

"You want me to spell it out?" He bends forward, face flushing red, and teeth protruding like he is going to eat me alive.

"Please. I don't remember anything about a ritual. What kind of ritual makes me kill a whole family?"

"A sacrificial ritual." He grits his teeth. "One that demands fourteen people dead."

"Fourteen?"

"Fourteen people sacrificed, and fourteen others making a deal."

"What deal?" I'm on my knees now, closer to the edge of the table, his voice pinching my ears, his spittle on my cheeks.

"The deal you did to save the devil."

"Devil? What nonsense are you talking about?"

The Chessmaster's anger subsides to the weakness in his knees. He falls down right next to me, about to cry his heart out. "The deal you did to save the Pillar."

Chapter 70

London

"Honk that bong!"

Having just arrived, Carter Pillar stood over a police car in the middle of the streets of London, celebrating in the most provocative ways. Everyone in London had fallen asleep because of the Chessmaster's curse, and only a few, probably immune to the curse, stood next to him.

When he'd first arrived, everyone was shocked with the sudden creepy silence in the city. Those who were still awake were in shock and grief, wondering who to ask for help.

But the Pillar, being the Pillar, had another point of view on the incident.

"Look at it this way," he told the people still awake. "The city is all ours. We can do whatever we want. You will never have a chance to do this in this miserable and densely populated London again."

"What would you have us do?" an old lady asked.

"Honk that bong!" he'd said, honking the horn of every car he came about.

"Honking is illegal!" the woman protested.

"And that's exactly the point." The Pillar winked.

It was only a few minutes before the others bought into his idea. Suddenly, Londoners went bonkers and began doing whatever was illegal.

Now the Pillar stood upon his limousine, watching them play golf and shooting balls against Parliament's windows, honking cars, and singing loudly in the streets.

"Go to the CCTV surveillance cameras!" the Pillar demanded. "Get it all recorded. This is an event like no other!"

Xian, on the other hand, not having arrived in America yet, didn't know where he was. He thought this was it, the place of freedom where he would be free to do whatever he wanted. So he took off his clothes and danced in the streets. At one point, he turned to the Pillar and said, "I love America!"

The Pillar didn't bother correcting him. He turned around and began walking to the most desired and important destination in London, at least according to him.

"Where are you going, Cao Pao Wong?" Xian inquired.

The Pillar took a moment to answer. He seemed thoughtful, thinking about too many things at once, and then said, "Time to finish something I started, Xian. It's all about choices, remember?"

Chapter 71

The last chess game, Chess City, Kalmykia

"I killed your family to save the Pillar?" I wipe the tears from my eyes.

"Fourteen people all in all." The Chessmaster sits back on his chair, collecting the chess pieces and putting them back in place. "You and the horrible Pillar."

"Why? Tell me. I need to know."

"Like you don't."

"Please. Please. Please. I need to know."

"You and the Pillar were the worst. You worked for Black Chess, aiding them in that eternal war between good and evil, trying to find the Six Keys."

"Okay?"

"The Pillar was never a Black Chess employee, not directly. He was nothing but a lowlife drug dealer living in Wonderland's forest, smoking his hookah and making more money."

"Really?"

"You, being the horrible Alice, needed his help in executing Black Chess's plan in finding the keys, which Lewis had hidden long ago."

"Why did he hide them? Why were they so important?"

"Don't play me and pretend you don't know!" The Chessmaster is losing it. "I'm never going to tell you what the keys are for."

"Never mind the keys. Tell me about the Pillar."

"The Pillar agreed to help you," the Chessmaster says. "Together you two were the most brutal monsters in Wonderland."

I shrug, speechless, wishing I could disappear and not hear the rest.

"However, the Pillar had a problem," the Chessmaster says. "The Cheshire Cat."

"What about him?"

"They'd always been rivals and hated each other in Wonderland. Not in a good versus bad way, but bad versus bad. They competed for who was the most evil, who killed and hurt more people. No one could ever stop them," the Chessmaster says. "But the Cheshire always topped the Pillar with his ability to possess souls. His nine lives."

"And?"

"The Pillar agreed to help you with finding the keys for Black Chess, under one condition. That you help him with a ritual that would grant him not nine lives, but fourteen, so he could top the Cheshire."

"You can't be serious." Strings of the rest of the story knit before my eyes. A jigsaw puzzle completing itself, too soon for me to take it all in.

"The ritual had you kill fourteen innocent people and use their blood or souls or whatever, with another fourteen people."

"Why?"

"It created a bond of fourteen souls and granted the Pillar fourteen lives." The Chessmaster has completed the reorganizing of the chessboard. "Fourteen Wonderlanders who have the blood of another fourteen innocent Wonderlanders inside them. Fourteen Wonderlanders who carried part of the Pillar's soul. So if he dies, he can use one of the others."

"That's the creepiest story I've ever heard."

"Not creepier than the Cheshire's grin," the Chessmaster remarks. "The fourteen had to carry the Pillar's chosen name. Carter Pillar. They were granted immortality and lived long enough to follow him into modern-day Oxford."

"They lived that long?"

"Carrying his fourteen lives so he can beat the Cheshire Cat."

"I don't believe this. The Pillar can be borderline bad, but not this evil."

"Why do you think he made you find the Cheshire Cat on your first mission?" the Chessmaster argues. "He wanted you to rid him of his nine lives, but you failed and the Cheshire got his mask back. This was the only reason to do so."

"You're lying."

"Really? How about the Executioner?"

"What about him?"

"You think you and the Pillar went to Mushroomland to save the world from him? This was the Pillar's plan all along."

"How so? This doesn't make the faintest of sense."

"The Executioner was one of the fourteen. And one of two people who carried the Pillar's soul and betrayed him."

"Betrayed him how?"

"He used another Wonderlastic ritual through which he managed to keep the soul and the Pillar's powers for himself," the Chessmaster says. "So the Pillar, in his vengeance, decided to kill them all, and the hell with immortality."

"And lose the fourteen powerful lives that easily?"

"You're acting like you don't know him. He is the devil in disguise. He has no friends. He hurt Fabiola. He played you and played the world. The fourteen's betrayal could only be met with death in the Pillar's book."

I try to connect the dots, and it strikes me that the Pillar only killed twelve people before being admitted to the asylum. Those, plus the Executioner, are thirteen. If the Chessmaster is right, then someone is missing. "Those are thirteen. One's missing."

"The one that got away." The Chessmaster laughs in a loud roar, the desire to burn the world showing in his eyes. "The one reason the Pillar is still there with you. The reason why he hasn't killed you yet. Because he was hoping you can lead him to the one who got away."

I sit opposite the Chessmaster, contemplating what to believe. Half of his story makes sense. The rest, no so much. I've been working on warming up to the Pillar for all these weeks, tolerating one thing after another. What really won me over was his belief in me, and helping me become a better person. How could this be an act? How?

"Let's say I believe you," I tell the Chessmaster. "How did you become Death?"

"Part of the ritual," he claims. "There was no Death before in Wonderland. Lewis, being the happy puppy and child inside a man that he was, wanted Wonderland to be deathless. But the ritual demanded the sacrifice to give something back to the forces of evil. And that was Death." He stares me in the eyes. "And, as the Pillar had killed my family, I accepted the position to create balance in the universe."

"And you killed Lewis."

"I did. But Lewis, in spite of being dead in his grave, always finds a way to stay alive in people's visions and dreams. I guess it's a power he has been granted by higher forces for writing a book like *Alice in Wonderland* that had so much effect through the years. Children must have handed him that kind of power. Don't ever underestimate children."

"But you just said the Pillar killed them, not me," I point out.

The Chessmaster shrugs. "I'm sure it was both of you, not just him."

"But you could be mistaken."

"Even if I am, only killing you will make me sleep better. These chess pieces will determine which one of us will live, Alice. Now get ready to play—and die."

Chapter 72

Inspector Dormouse was back in Tom's car. He'd picked the keys from the sleeping man's pocket and walked the Tom Quad all alone, the only man awake in this neighborhood. He plugged the flash drive into the car's stereo and listened.

The recorded sessions were really long, mostly boring, but Dormouse caught a few slip-ups here and there. The story was peeling itself easily.

Back in Wonderland, the Pillar had conspired with Alice to create fourteen lives with an unholy ritual. The Pillar and the Cheshire turned out to be lifelong nemeses, who, in spite of the significance of the Wonderland Wars, were purely shameless monsters who cared for no one but themselves.

There may have been a long-lasting war between good and evil, personified in the Inklings and Black Chess, but there was another great war between the Pillar and the Cheshire. A war of souls. Who possessed more lives? The Cheshire, being a cat, had been granted nine lives through an ancient mask, which Lewis once tried to scatter all over the world. The Pillar's technique was that of being a caterpillar, morphing into a cocoon then a chrysalis and then a butterfly, which gave him a lifespan of four short lives. The Pillar wanted much more.

The recording also showed the Pillar's plan to kill the fourteen after two of them betrayed him by taking their powers into their own hands, and the other twelve thinking it over.

Dormouse couldn't fathom the carnage of evil in this world, let alone Wonderland. Wasn't it supposed to be the children's friendly place with all the cute rabbits and enchanting roses? What made it that way? Was this Carroll's plan, or did something evil slip from this beautiful creation?

How in heaven's name did our beloved and enchanting childhood turn into this bloodbath of adulthood?

Dormouse didn't know what to do. It was all clear now. But somehow he had a soft spot for Alice. First, she reminded him of his daughter. In fact, she reminded him of all the struggling teenage daughters in his neighborhood. Those girls fighting for their own identities in a world that imposed nonsensical rules and obligations to grow up.

What if every teenage girl from around the block had the power to save the world? Which teacher or parent in this scary world outside would ever notice?

Inspector Dormouse didn't feel like sleeping now. It was the Pillar he had to get, at all costs. This evil embodiment of darkness. He had to be put back in the asylum—or prison.

But where would the inspector start?

A question with a simple answer that he suddenly heard on the recording. One of the fourteen people was explaining why the Pillar couldn't track number fourteen.

It turned out that the mysterious Mr. Fourteen, with a plan to beat the devil, longed for the help of another devil. The Cheshire.

Inspector Dormouse chuckled listening to this. Everything was really messed up in this story.

Mr. Fourteen asked the Cheshire to help him. Why? Because it turned out that the Pillar, having decided on killing them, had to kill each and every one of them. Kill only thirteen and the ritual was reversed, meaning the Pillar's life's expectancy was lessened and shortened. That was why the

Pillar was having a skin problem, a rare disease that he kept secret.

Of course, the Cheshire liked the idea, and granted Mr. Fourteen the power of splitting his soul in two—it was the best the Cheshire could do, but it was more than enough.

Doing so, apparently so many years ago, helped Mr. Fourteen have two bodies, one that traveled abroad and left the continent completely, and the other that still lived in London, under a disguise and different name.

The Cheshire's plan was to delude the Pillar into killing the one in London, making him think he was safe, and then he'd die suddenly without even knowing it.

"This isn't Wonderland," Dormouse told himself. "This is London's Chainsaw Massacre tripled by Hannibal Lecter's madness. In short, this is a British horror story."

In the end, Inspector Dormouse needed a lead. Something in the recording that would give a clue to where to find Mr. Fourteen, because, thinking logically, this was why the Pillar had come back to London all of a sudden, instead of helping Alice.

The Pillar was about to kill Mr. Fourteen, and Inspector Dormouse was ready to stop that from happening.

Chapter 73

The last chess game, Chess City, Kalmykia

Whatever I do or say to apologize, there is no escaping from the Chessmaster's game. And how in the world can I win or save the world from him? Why is it even my burden to do so when I've been the worst person in the world in the past?

"Ready, darling?" The Chessmaster's dark tone returns tenfold. "Don't ever think that the pain I've been through made me weaker. Don't ever think I have a soft spot and will back off any moment. Being Death for all those years made me heartless, and there is only one joy left in my life: to see you suffer."

"Why not ask to play against the Pillar?" I ask.

"I took care of the Pillar long ago," he says. "I even ignored it when he escaped Chess City and left you behind. He is dying, only he doesn't know it. I made sure he'd take the bait."

"I thought it was me who was going to kill him," I say. "He read it in the future."

"But of course it was you who killed him—will kill him. You just don't know it. He doesn't know it."

"How will I kill him if I die today?"

"People plant the seed of death in others long before anyone knows it, darling," the Chessmaster says. "You think you have to pull the trigger to do so. Start playing, because you're wasting my time."

I stare with a blank mind at the table, then at the chess pieces, then at the cups of poison. There is no way I can survive this.

A man with a tray arrives with a complimentary drink all of a sudden. I glance at the Chessmaster to see if he is going to object, but he doesn't.

"A complimentary drink…" The Chessmaster brushes the left side of his mustache. "Of death." He laughs. "I'm always a good host. Never kill without a good last meal or drink. I'll even pay for your coffin."

None of the Chessmaster's show unsettles me. In fact, I'm most curious about the man offering me the drink on the tray. Because it's a Red. My guardian angel. The Dude.

"Didn't know Reds work for you," I tell the Chessmaster.

"They're vulgar killing machines who would do anything for money," the Chessmaster says. "I'm happy they conceal their faces under their hoods, because I'm sure they're pretty ugly."

But I don't think my Red is ugly, because I can feel it—he is my guardian angel.

I reach for the glass, trying to meet his unseen eyes. He doesn't say anything, but nods toward the glass. I squint, not sure what he is implying. He must be here to help me somehow.

Then, when he nods again, I see it. He is nodding at the bottom of the glass. There is a napkin, a round one, sticking out at the bottom. It's a message. Another note. Now I certainly know it's him.

Remember: "He Who Laughs Last" & "That you will die when you say so."

I lift my head up and shrug, wishing the Red would explain further. But he nods, takes the glass back, and leaves.

Did he just give me a clue how to win this game? And how come those are the Pillar's words? "He Who Laughs Last" was the Pillar's theory in killing the giant. How can I implement this in the game of chess I'm about to play?

Then there is the silly "I will die when I say so," those words the Pillar was feeding to the old people in the hospice.

Are those really the solution to my struggle? I can trust the Red, my guardian, but do I want to take advice from the Pillar after all I just heard about him?

Chapter 74

The Vatican

The Cheshire watched the people of the Vatican panic, confused about who would take the deceased Pope's place. Though he knew there were prolonged and accurate processes to elect a new one, there seemed to be an unexplained urgency to find a new Pope immediately. Maybe because the Vatican hadn't gone to sleep yet. They needed a Pope before that happened.

None of this was of interest to the Cheshire, though. He'd just flown over to amuse himself. After all, he was bored, unable to find one soul to possess and stick to—and he'd watched so many movies that he couldn't meow anymore.

Needing to make a phone call, he possessed the first old lady with a mobile he came across. She wore a terrible perfume that he hated, but he tolerated it until he finished the call.

"Did the Pillar find Mr. Fourteen?" the Cheshire asked.

"Looks like it," the voice at the other end of the line said.

"The one in London?"

"Yes."

"Not the other Mr. Fourteen?"

"No, only the one in London."

"Looks good," the Cheshire said in the woman's voice. "The plan is on. He will find the one in London and kill him, then stop looking. Soon, he will die of his illness without knowing it, and I get rid of him forever."

"It seems like you will also get rid of Alice. The Chessmaster has her cornered."

"So he found Carroll's Knight."

"He did."

The Cheshire grinned. It was such an unsettling grin that a few people stepped away from the old woman. "Then Alice is dead, too. She can't win against the Chessmaster."

"It's a beautiful day, Chesh."

"Beautiful indeed. Two of my enemies dead in one day, after all these years." The Cheshire hung up and walked out of the Vatican.

He found a shortcut through an empty and darkened alley, so he took it, only to be stopped by a black figure in the dark.

"Oh." The Cheshire shrugged, lowering the woman's head.

"Didn't expect me?" the man said in a baritone voice.

"No, but it's always a pleasure to meet you, Mr. Jay."

"I don't show myself much, but I thought we could use a little talk."

"Whatever you ask."

"I know you're not a Black Chess employee, and that you have interests of your own, so I never pressured you into joining."

"That's right, sir. I'm most irritated with the Queen of Hearts. I don't think I can work with her in the same place, ever."

"Understood."

"Besides, you're all interested in this Wonderland War, and I'm just a cat. I want to have fun."

"And you want to crush your enemies. I just learned about your rivalry with the Pillar. The fourteen souls."

"You did?" the Cheshire said. "Well, me and the Pillar go way back."

"I know."

"Besides, I think not only will he die soon, but Alice, too."

Mr. Jay stood silent, his breathing the soundtrack of a horror movie. "I don't want Alice to die."

"I just figured out the stupidity of my implication. I'm most sorry." The Cheshire bowed his head a little lower.

"But I'm also not concerned with Alice's safety."

"Pardon me?"

"Alice is my best employee. She will beat the Chessmaster."

"But that's impossible."

"Nothing's impossible with my dark little angel," Mr. Jay said. "I'm not here to talk about her. I'm here to talk about you."

"Me?"

"It's time you stick to one soul, or you'll lose your mind."

The Cheshire purred. Mr. Jay always knew how to see through him.

"I'm not going to ask you to work for me, but I will hand you a soul you have no means of possessing. How about that?"

The Cheshire grinned. He was thinking it was a Wonderlander—someone other than the obnoxious Queen. "Who?"

"Let me show you," Mr. Jay said.

Chapter 75

The last chess game, Chess City, Kalmykia

The Chessmaster is unbeatable. Two moves now, and two drinks, and I feel like I'm going to lose after the next.

"Afraid?" The Chessmaster grins.

"I prefer not to talk while playing."

"But we know you're not playing, Alice. You're dying."

"Then I'd prefer to keep the last minutes of my life to myself."

"They're hardly minutes. I can finish you in much less time."

"How so, when you can't make your move before I make my third?"

"Then make your third move, drink the poison, and move on."

His last words ring in the back of my head. I realize that to win this game, I can't just keep on playing. It is a fool's hope that something will suddenly happen and save me.

In my mind, the Pillar's words pop up in the back of my head. *He Who Laughs Last. It's an old None Fu trick.*

My mind flashes to a memory from the hole in Tibet. I see the Pillar fight the giant again, bluntly asking him to hit him more and more until the giant has lost confidence in himself, and just when he does, the Pillar attacks him, full throttle.

I remember telling myself I could never imitate the Pillar's move, but I have no choice but consider it now. This is what the Red wrote for me on the napkin.

But how can I laugh last with the Chessmaster? How can I play like I don't care and I am not going to lose until my moment comes and I strike back?

I scratch my head. It's impossible, because striking back in this game means making a bold, brilliant chess move, and I know I can't.

Think, Alice. Think.

"Ready for your third move?" the Chessmaster asks.

"No, I'm not," I say. "But maybe I could use your help."

His suspicious look troubles me. He senses I'm onto something. I am, but the funny thing is, I don't know what it is either.

"Why would you think I would advise you on a good move?" he asks.

"I didn't say you would do that," I say. "But since I'm losing anyway, you might want to amuse yourself with my moves. Maybe use a move that makes me look like a total fool."

"I like that." He nods and reaches for my knight.

Knight, Alice, why did he reach for your knight? Remember when the Pillar said he'd prefer to be a knight in a chess game? *Because they'll never see you coming.*

"Just a second." I stop the Chessmaster, buying myself some time.

"What now? Changed your mind?"

"Actually, no, but I thought we could spice up the game a little."

"Why would I want to do that?"

Why, Alice, why?

"Because of the audience behind me." I point over my shoulder. "They need some entertainment."

A few men and women in the dark agree.

"You see?" I say. "They don't want to watch a game where they know I will just die in the end."

"Then what do they want to watch?"

"A game where there is the slightest possibility I will win. Just a little bit."

"I can't help you with that," the Chessmaster says. "It's you who is dumb, not me."

"Yes, but you could play on my behalf."

"This is what I was about to do when you stopped me."

"But you could play a brilliant move on my behalf, not a bad one," I say.

"Again, why would I do that?"

"To show your audience how you can excel and win, even with such a brilliant move."

The Chessmaster's smile broadens. He likes it. He just bit into a wasp's nest without knowing it. Even when I'm only buying time, not knowing what to do.

And then he makes a third move on my behalf.

Chapter 76

This obliges me to drink my third drink. I haven't felt anything from the last two, but the third is definitely dizzying. That's not good; I need my mind alert to think of something else.

Surprisingly, the Chessmaster struggles with topping his own move. A few members of the unseen crowd hiss with wonder. The Chessmaster tenses.

A few minutes later, I see him sweat. Is he really that stupid, or hasn't he played against his ego before?

But finally he manages and responds to his own move.

"Brilliant!" a few members of the audience hail.

"Now I should play your fourth move," he tells me.

And just right there, when his hand reaches for my fourth move, I get hit with a lightning bolt in my head. I immediately stop his hand.

"What now?"

"I think I can make my next move," I declare.

"Is that so?"

"I think I can beat you," I say.

"Really? Again? Do you really think you have the slightest idea what you are talking about?"

"I think I do."

The audience members in the dark gasp.

"Come on," the Chessmaster says. "You don't really believe she can—"

I interrupt him with my next move. The winner's move.

The Chessmaster squints at it. His face dims. His forehead knots.

Then the Chessmaster bursts into uncontrollable laughter. "Do you have any idea what you just did?" He points at the chessboard. "You're so easy, you have no idea."

"Why?" I act surprised, afraid, worried, and shocked.

"You just handed me an early win with your move," he says.

"You can't be serious."

"I am. You totally lost it. This is the worst move possible. I can checkmate you right now."

I stop a small, sneaky smile from shaping on the corners of my lips. Unfortunately, he catches it.

"Wait." He leans back. "You have a bigger plan, don't you?"

I dim my face and tense my shoulders on purpose. "I wish I had. I really thought this was the best move."

"Really?" He thinks it over. "You know, none of the world leaders I played with, no matter how bad at chess they were, made such a bad move."

"Oh." I cup my mouth with my hands. "Did I do that badly?"

"You could have shot yourself in Russian roulette and never done this badly."

"Can you please give me a chance to correct it?" I plead, reaching for his hands.

The Chessmaster pushes them away. "Of course not. You know why? Because your move is so bad, I have no other move but to checkmate you. I mean, literally, I have no other option but to end the game now."

As I'm still pleading with him, he, still enraged, unthinkingly reaches for his favorite knight and checkmates me.

The crowd behind me claps and hails and chirps with enthusiasm, cameras flashing from all around.

"This is the moment I've been waiting for," he tells me, mirth wrapping his soul. "I've killed you, Alice."

That's when I sit back, cross one leg over another, place my elbow on the rim of the chair, and glance with disgust at him.

The Chessmaster doesn't sense at first what has really happened here, but some in the audience do. They let out a series of uncontrollable shrieks, saying, "She tricked him!"

The Chessmaster's face knots so tightly I think he's going to bleed. He stares at the chess pieces, the checkmated king, and doesn't get it. What's the fuss about? Why is the audience saying that the little girl from Wonderland tricked him?

Then his eyes shift toward the poison cups.

I seize the moment and reach for my fourth cup and gulp it with all the ease in the world. It does drive me crazy and makes me dizzy, but I don't show it, because I'm in for the grand prize: saving the world.

"You tricked me." The Chessmaster slumps back in his chair. "You little b—"

"Save the swearing for when you burn in hell," I tell him, remembering what the Pillar taught me. "I made you play with my rules, not yours."

"Who taught you such a trick? Why hasn't anyone thought of it before?"

"Because they're afraid of you. You're the terrorist who bombs a building with innocent people because he's been hurt in the past. You force people to play your game by scaring them." I am so excited I can't even catch my breath. "And all I had to do was play my game, not yours."

"By making me think you made your best move when in fact it was deliberately your intention to make your worst." The Chessmaster moans, knowing his time has come.

"Exactly," I say. "You forced me in a game where I have to try winning in a losing war; where, when I lose in the end, I have no choice but to drink the seventh poisoned cup that will kill me."

"And you fooled me by losing earlier and not buying into my game." The Chessmaster is amazed but saddened and disappointed with this whole outcome. "Now that you made the most stupid move in history, I had no choice but to checkmate you in the fourth round."

"Stupidity is so underrated."

"And by recklessly checkmating you in the fourth round, you will never reach the seventh cup, and you will simply not die," he says. "You bought yourself out of hell by being a moron."

"I prefer being called mad."

"And that's not all." The Chessmaster nails his own coffin with his last words: "Having been unable to kill you, I'm obliged to drink all seven cups, even though I checkmated you. It's the rules of the game."

"Let me just correct that part. In reality, I checkmated you. Kinda kicked you in the balls, wrapped you up in choking coils made out of your anger, and rolled you down the rabbit hole of hell."

The Reds in the place crash onto the stage and force the Chessmaster to drink the seven cups of poison.

I watch him give in, the audience behind me applauding, reminding myself of the man who taught me this trick.

The Pillar.

With my Red guardian reminding me of the technique written on the napkin, I was the one who laughed last. I didn't buy into the Chessmaster's game, made him think he was winning, and struck when it was hot.

Now that I've practiced what I've learned and saved the world, I have to finish my masterpiece with a few last words. Words I was taught by the Pillar, whom everyone says is a devil.

A broad smile, a euphoric feeling of transcendence, and a breeze of hope caress me as I stand above the Chessmaster, Death himself, and tell him,

"I will die when I say so!"

Chapter 77

London

Inspector Dormouse had finally reached the address where Mr. Fourteen resided. He'd managed to extract it from the conversations in the recordings and had driven from Oxford to London, hoping he wasn't too late.

He stopped the car by a place called Lifespan, a hospice where Mr. Fourteen hid, pretending he was a dying man, just to stay away from the Pillar's wrath.

With everyone asleep, the lazy inspector stepped up and entered the main hall. He pushed the sleeping nurse aside and flipped through the guests' names. He'd learned the name from the recordings too.

There he was, a resident in a private room on the sixth floor.

Dormouse hurried to the lift but found it dead. Maybe the lifts had fallen asleep too.

He had to struggle with the misfortune and pain of climbing up the stairs. Gosh, six storeys?

Inspector Dormouse was incredibly out of shape. The last time he had climbed six storeys must have been in his sleep.

Three floors up, panting and wheezing and feeling his limbs fall apart, he fell asleep again. He just couldn't resist it.

A few minutes later he woke up, shocked and disappointed with himself. What if the Pillar had reached Mr. Fourteen earlier?

Like a slow-chugging locomotive, the inspector trudged step after step, now coughing out thick fumes he preferred not to look at.

Finally, there he was. On the sixth floor. A few strides ahead and he'd be inside Mr. Fourteen's room—even if he'd found him asleep, he would still be able to protect him.

But first, Dormouse needed to drink. He stopped by the cooler in the corridor and gulped water, wetting his shirt and pants in the process of his slurping.

Fresh now, he still had to tie the loosened laces on his shoes, and then he approached the room.

He knocked once but no one answered. Mr. Fourteen was unquestionably asleep.

But what was that blood seeping from under the door?

Enraged, Inspector Dormouse kicked open the door into a dark room.

A switch flicked by the opposite wall. A faint yellow light that only showed two things: a man dead on the floor, probably Mr. Fourteen, and the Pillar with a gun in his hand, sitting nonchalantly under the yellow light.

"Too late, inspector." The Pillar smirked.

"You killed him," Dormouse said. "You killed Mr. Fourteen."

"Had to be done," the Pillar said. "It took me a long time to find him."

"What kind of beast are you?"

"Call it what you want. I made my choice."

"You call killing an innocent man a choice?"

"What makes you think he is so innocent?"

"I know all about you, Pillar. I know about your deal. You and Alice. The ritual to gain more lives than the Cheshire."

"Really?" the Pillar said. "Is that what you know?"

"You killed the Fourteen because they betrayed you and wouldn't let you collect your souls."

"That's one side of the story." The Pillar rubbed something inside his ear with his pinky, his other hand gripping the gun, pointed at the inspector.

"There is no other side to it," Dormouse said. "You will not walk out of this building alive."

"I came and went as I pleased in the asylum. No one could ever stop me," the Pillar said. "Besides, you should really lower your voice, inspector. Everyone's asleep."

"You got that part wrong, professor." Dormouse smiled victoriously, as the people in the hall were starting to wake up. "Because Alice killed the Chessmaster. People are about to wake up."

And for all the conflicting reasons in the world, Dormouse saw the Pillar smiling in broad lines, his eyes wide, and it looked like his heart was fluttering. Dormouse didn't know what to make of this. If the Pillar was this brutal beast, how come he was so happy Alice was still alive?

Chapter 78

The last chess game, Chess City, Kalmykia

"You think you beat me?" The Chessmaster writhed on the ground, gasping his last few breaths. "I never lose."

"Don't fight it," I tell him. "The world is a better place without you. The world is safe now."

"And ironically, you'll be the hero?"

"Trust me, no one ever thinks I'm the hero. I'm a nineteen-year-old mad girl at best. Most of my boyfriends die, or I make silent sacrifices for them. I have no friends. Neither do I have idols. Everything around me is a purple haze of madness, but you know what? I save a few people from time to time."

"You killed my family. You're not supposed to win."

"Even if I did, I'm really, really sorry, but that wasn't me. That was someone else."

"I still can't believe I'm dying after all these years of planning to get you and the Pillar," he slurs, coughing.

I kneel down beside him. "About the Pillar," I say. "How come the Executioner was one of the Fourteen when I saw the Pillar missing two fingers, like every other child the Executioner enslaved in Mushroomland?"

"What do you mean?"

"I mean, it seems like the Pillar was a man, enslaved by the Executioner as a kid in Colombia at some point," I say. "Even though the whole timeline is messed up, it still seems to me the Executioner tortured the Pillar as a kid."

"You've got it all wrong."

"Maybe it's you who is lying and made it all up." I want to believe the Pillar isn't that bad. I really want to.

"You don't get it." The Chessmaster's eyelids flutter. "The Pillar used to meet the Fourteen in a secret place underneath Oxford, in the kitchen. There is a reckless cook called Chopin who accidentally chops off people's fingers. He even chopped his own finger once."

"So?"

"The Pillar once caught him eavesdropping. They had a fight. Chopin escaped, and chopped off the Pillar's two fingers on the way out."

"You expect me to believe this story?"

"I don't expect anything from you." The Chessmaster's eyes fling open with all the power left in him. "It's you who is blind. It's you who wants to believe the Pillar is a good man. Can't you see?"

"No, I can't," I say. "I could never see the Pillar wanting to mass-murder people. It's the monsters like you I come across each week who do this."

"What if I can prove it to you?" The Chessmaster grips my arm. His need to tell me something far outweighs his weakness due to the poison he just gulped.

"What is it?" Something tells me I don't want to hear it.

"Say my name," he demands.

"Pardon me?"

"Say my name, Alice."

"Okay, if that's your last wish. You're the Chessmaster."

"Not that name." His grip tightens. "My real name."

"Ah, that. Your Russian name." I try to recall it. "What was it? Yes, your name is Vozchik Stolb. Why?"

"Can't you see what my name means?"

"I'm not into Russian."

"Vozchik is a rough Russian translation of the word *Carter* in English," he begins, and the world begins to spin again. "Stolb means…"

"Pillar," I finish it for him. "You're one of the Fourteen."

"Yes." The Chessmaster winces. He is determined to tell me, though. "That's why I told you I've made sure he dies. I split my soul into two with the Cheshire's help. He is after the one in London, not knowing I exist."

Even though I'm shocked, I have to give the Chessmaster the bad news. "I'm sorry, but you really underestimate the Pillar," I tell him. "Do you really think he doesn't know who you are? The Pillar planned this all along. That's why he left for London, and paved the way for me to kill you here."

The Chessmaster's dying eyes are in flames. He's shocked to hear about the genius Pillar, who has fooled him, me, and the world. I am as shocked as him, having finally tied the knots of the puzzle. Who is this man called Carter Pillar, and why is he doing this?

"What are you telling me?" the Chessmaster says.

"I'm telling you if there is one man who played Chess with God and won, then it's not you, but the Pillar." I'm not sure what to think of the Pillar. Maybe the premonition about me killing him in the future is real. Hell, it begins to feel like a must.

"Damn you, Alice and the Pillar!" The Chessmaster lets go of me as I stand up.

I prefer to have the Pillar at my back. There is no point in being sentimental. I'm a bad girl who is determined to do good things and save the world from the worst kind of evil. To do so, I have to make choices, like killing a man I may have once hurt—if it wasn't the Pillar, and he just pulled me into the story somehow—to save so many lives. In my book it's not who you were yesterday. It's who you are today.

And though the tables have turned, the Chessmaster with his pain is the villain today, and I'm trying to save lives.

It's a grey truth. Colorless, confusing, and borderline unethical. But it's a truth that saves innocent people's lives.

"Damn you, Alice!" The Chessmaster won't give up before he dies, expressing his hatred toward me.

But I have no time for him. I need to find the Pillar, and in case he turns out to be that evil genius, I will have to believe that in the future I kill him.

The Red, my guardian angel, stands before me and pats me on the shoulder. In his hands, I see my Tiger Lily.

Note: *I knew it meant much to you, so I kept it safe. You did well, Alice. You did the right thing.*

"Why are you sure?" I ask, hugging the pot.

Because I believe in you. And look, the people in the world are awake. You helped them open their eyes. Maybe someday they will see how great you are.

"You think I'm great?" I ask. "Why do you believe in me so much? Who are you?"

I'm the one who will guard you until you grow old, become a mother and grandma with wrinkles on your face, and have arthritis climbing on your back like a monkey.

"Not the best choice of words." I chuckle.

It's not about the words you hear, it's about what you feel, Alice.

"Seriously," I say. "Who are you? Are you my future husband, trying to get into my heart?"

The Dude doesn't answer me.

"Wait. Are you Jack? Please tell me you're Jack."

The Dude doesn't answer again, but pushes a sword into my hand.

It was Fabiola's Vorpal sword. It's yours now.

"Who gave it to you?" I grip the sword with Fabiola's blood fresh on it.

She is alive. She told me to give it to you. Now go get the Pillar, if he does deserve to die.

The Dude disappears into the crowd, cameras still flashing everywhere, TV spreading the news of the world having been saved, but no one mentions my name.

On my way out to find the Pillar, the Chessmaster insists on cursing me. This time, it's a bit different. "Damn you, Alice. Damn you...and your family."

This cements my feet to the ground. "I have no family," I say without turning. "Lorina, Edith, and their mysterious mother aren't my family."

The Chessmaster laughs through his coughing and last breaths. "Oh, Lord in heaven. She doesn't know."

I hurl back and part the people in my space, stooping over his body, now on the ambulance's stretcher. "What don't I know?"

"You don't know who your family is, Alice," he says. "I thought you were playing me, but you really don't remember your family."

I pull him closer to me by the neck, disgusted by the breath coming out of his foul mouth. "I have a family? A biological family, you mean?"

"Of course." His eyes are glimmering with some sort of mocking victory. "Your family, Alice. They're the reason why you became who you are after the circus."

He doesn't stop laughing. As if my pain, and his amusement, gave him the means to live again. "It turns out I really never lose a game of chess," he says. "Because I will die without telling about them. I will take it to my grave, and I will always be the Chessmaster who never loses."

In spite of me holding on to him, wanting to squeeze out answers, the soul inside him departs his body. It's like he's been waiting for this last moment to declare his win, and leave me hopeless, helpless, and lost without knowing about my real family.

Chapter 79

Lifespan Hospice, London

Inspector Dormouse was still intoxicated with the Pillar's happiness over Alice's survival. It even seemed like a weak point in the professor's attitude, enough to encourage Dormouse to attack him. But the inspector's out-of-shape body wasn't going to help.

"Close the door behind you," the Pillar demanded. "Before everyone wakes up."

Dormouse couldn't oppose the notorious monster by the name of Carter Pillar.

"Step in closer," the Pillar said.

Dormouse did, trying to figure out what was going on. There was this one possibility. A flicker of a thought. A slice of an assumption. A far-fetched idea he didn't want to think about. Driving all the way from Oxford to London, he'd been thinking about it. He just couldn't swallow it.

Now, staring right into the Pillar's face, the idea surfaced. The Pillar wasn't the most honest of men; his moral code was shabby, and to the police force he was a serial killer. But if there was one quality about the Pillar, one which Inspector Dormouse had witnessed over and over again, it was this: the Pillar cared about Alice. He would die for her.

The look on the Pillar's face simply exposed him. And Dormouse, being a father, knew how precious a look it was, unconditionally caring about someone.

"Who are you, Professor Pillar?" Dormouse had to ask.

Half of the Pillar's face shone in the weak yellow under a lamp. The other half loomed behind the dark. He looked like a ghost, one who'd disappear any moment, but leave his scent behind, forever haunting you—in good ways and in bad.

"I will give you the precious chance to leave this place right now," the Pillar said. "I will never hurt you. All you have to do is go back to your sleepy life and never mention whatever you've discovered. Believe me, you don't want to know the truth."

Dormouse hesitated.

"Go back to your daughter, inspector," the Pillar advised. "I'm not a sentimental man, and will shoot you dead if you dig deeper into things you shouldn't."

Inspector Dormouse nodded, turned around, and paced toward the door. What was he really doing here, digging into the secrets of Wonderland? He was better off going back home, enjoying a nap among his family members who loved him—and were much saner than the world outside.

Inspector Dormouse even made it so far as to grip the doorknob on his way out. But then the conclusion hit him hard, a revelation so intense and surprising he feared he'd never be able to sleep again.

He turned around and faced the Pillar. "Oh, holy lord of rings," he said. "I know who you are."

The Pillar tilted his head with pursed lips. He even shook his head. "Don't do it, Dormouse. Don't think too much. It may cost you more than you can handle."

"Let me rephrase it," Dormouse insisted, unable to suppress his thoughts. "All of us have been mistaken from the beginning, questioning who you really were."

The Pillar said nothing.

"We were asking the wrong question," Inspector Dormouse said. "The right question was who you weren't. And who you aren't."

The Pillar squeezed his eyes shut and let out a long sigh. He gritted his teeth, his hand tightening on the gun. "Don't say it, Dormouse. Just leave."

But Dormouse's excitement and curiosity got the best of him. "You're not the Pillar. You have no relation to the monster Carter Chrysalis Cocoon Pillar whatsoever."

The Pillar opened his eyes, looking angry, like a hangman sad he had to pull the lever, and pointed the gun at the inspector.

"In the name of Wonderland, Alice, Lewis Carroll, and all the mad people in the world," Dormouse said. "Who are you?"

"I'm the one who unfortunately needs to put you to sleep—forever," the Pillar said, and shot him dead.

The END...

Alice will return in Family (Insanity 7)

Thank You

Thank you for purchasing and downloading *Checkmate*. The only book in the series without an epilogue—or two. Reason? I didn't want to prepare you for the surprises. *"Oh, now to the epilogue, the big reveal!"* I wanted the big reveals to hit you earlier than expected. I hope it worked.

Checkmate is the Insanity book I'm proudest of so far, and that's because it's a purely organic book, meaning events happened because characters said so, and because the logical turn of events and circumstances forced the story to go this way. After knowing about her past, Alice needed to prove to herself she can stand up to Black Chess by taking the harshest of decisions, and the Pillar, well, we need to know who the heck he is and what he really wants with her. All those chapters you've just read—trust me, I was only a means to writing them, but they developed on their own. I really liked that.

However, there was an epilogue, tying the loose end in the Cheshire's story after meeting Mr. Jay, but I chopped it out because I didn't want you to know who the Cheshire will possess from now, not in this book. It will be explained in *Family*, the next book in the series. In many ways, *Family* is a continuation of *Checkmate*.

All puzzles and landmarks mentioned are real, and so are the facts— I'm always happy when I receive emails from readers who've visited these places because of the books.

Characters like Mr. Paperwhite and Father Williams are Lewis Carroll's inventions. However, characters like Chopin the Chopper are mine (he just popped up on the screen and wouldn't let go, and, frankly, I dared not chop him out of the story, because I feared for my fingers).

Last but not least, I can't express how much I enjoy writing this series. I probably enjoy writing it more than any of you enjoy reading it.

Don't miss the Pinterest page, where you can see all the places and riddles Alice and Pillar visited (I've updated it, so there are whole new places to see).

You can access it HERE (Pinterest) or HERE (Instagram)

Family (Insanity 7) will be released soon, so please stay tuned to my Facebook Page:

http://Facebook.com/camjace

or

http://cameronjace.com for more information.

If you have a question, please message me on Facebook; I love connecting with all of my readers, because without you, none of this would be possible.

Thank you, for sharing this mad journey with me,

Cam

About the Author

The part that matters:

Cameron Jace is a storykiller. He kills older stories and resurrects them into larger-than-life tales weaved within facts and fiction. With a knack for collecting out-of-print books, he is fascinated with folklore and those who wrote it. He wonders if it's possible to track back to the first story ever told.

The part that is nothing but propaganda:

Cameron is the bestselling author of the Grimm Diaries series and the Insanity series. Three of his books made Amazon's Top 100 Customer Favorites books for 2013. He is a graduate of the College of Architecture, but prefers building a fortress of imagination over a house. Cameron lives in California with his girlfriend. He loves to hear from you:

Via email: camjace@hotmail.com
Twitter: @cameronjace
Facebook: facebook.com/camjace
Instagram: instagram.com/storykiller
Snapchat: Storykiller
Web: http://www.cameronjace.com
Goodreads: goodreads.com/CameronJace

Made in the USA
San Bernardino, CA
28 October 2017